For Maureen, Ali, and Cait.
You were right!
—*A.H.*

Acknowledgements

I am very grateful to my editor, Ann Featherstone, whose insight and thoroughness have greatly improved this story; and to Gail Winskill at Fitzhenry & Whiteside for her constant support and encouragement. I owe a special debt of gratitude to Justin Sofio, driver for the Mathiasen Motorsports/RLM Investments Formula Atlantic team in California, and to Cam Binder of Binder Racing in Calgary. Justin and Cam graciously adopted me as a crew member, patiently answered all of my technical questions about their Swift 008 race car, and even gave me an official team hat.

Chapter 1

Wakeup Toronto!

The next time I'm asked to be on a TV show, I'll try not to run over the host with my race car. As a rookie driver in the North American Formula Atlantic Championship, I found that television exposure was a great chance to promote our young team and our new sponsor, DynaSport Industries. I saw it as a golden opportunity to show off the shimmering candy-apple red of our number 28 Swift Formula Atlantic car, and to impress the viewers with just how professional we were. I'd rehearsed all of the correct pro race driver answers, polished my helmet, and pressed my driving suit twice. I thought I was prepared for anything. I was wrong.

The Atlantic series organizers had decided to promote the next race around the streets of Toronto by having some of the leading drivers appear on local TV shows during race week. As our team had nearly won the last race in Milwaukee two weeks ago, we were picked. Along with our team manager, Caroline Grant, I was scheduled to appear on the number-one morning television breakfast show, "Wakeup Toronto!" from 6:00 to 9:00 a.m. That meant that we had to get ourselves and the race car to the station by 5:00 a.m., wheel the Swift into the studio, go over the show's format, and then wait until we were on.

"Wakeup Toronto!" did the usual daily news, weather, sports, and traffic updates, as well as some features that they thought viewers would find interesting. We were scheduled to follow a guy who had built a medieval battering ram to demolish his garage, and two elderly, blue-haired ladies who had taught their budgies to chirp along to a disco version of "The Skater's Waltz." Some folks in southern Ontario seemed to have a lot of spare time.

The TV studio was huge and had been converted from an old movie theater. The main set looked up at thirty rows of seats separated by a wide middle aisle. At 5:30 a.m. the doors opened, and in rushed a live audience of about 500 people, who had actually lined up before dawn to get a seat. Like I said, lots of spare time. At 5:45, Caroline and I were introduced to the two hosts of the show, Brittany and Steve, who had been telling lame hockey jokes to the audience. Both in their mid twenties, they looked like a matched set of aerobics-instructor dolls with perfect salon tans, brilliantly polished teeth, and designer clothes.

Steve wore a loose-fitting dark suit with a black shirt, a burgundy tie, and about half a quart of gel to preserve the spikes in his short blond hair. Brittany, who apparently had nicer legs than Steve, wore a short blue dress and lots of silver and turquoise jewelry. And she held back her mane of frizzy red hair with small plastic hairclips shaped like sharks. They were both incredibly bubbly and upbeat, completely pumped with their roles as talk-show hosts. Caroline was grinning and full of energy herself as she did the introductions.

"Steve and Brittany, I'm Caroline Grant, DynaSport Motorsport's team manager. Meet Eddie Stewart, the fastest rookie in the North American Formula Atlantic series."

I shook hands with Steve and put on my best fast-rookie smile. I could tell that Brittany was instantly impressed. With the race car.

"I just *love* this car! It's like, you know, just so cool. I think; don't you, Steve?"

Steve nodded vigorously. "Brittany, you are so

right! Hey! Hold on! Idea! Idea, Brittany!"

"Yes! Go, Steve!" Brittany gasped.

"I know you're gonna hate this, Britt, but what if Evelyn here—"

"That's Caroline," I corrected him.

"Caroline! Right! Thanks, Teddy."

"Eddie."

"Eddie! Hey, sorry, man! OK, anyway, so, listen to this. What if we put the race car in the audience, push it all the way up the center aisle, right to the top. Caroline climbs in, and here's the best part. We introduce them, Eddie gives her a push, and she rolls that baby right down the aisle and onto the set!"

Brittany clapped her hands with glee. "Yes! Steve, that would be so, like, you know, so—"

"Amazing?" Steve suggested helpfully.

"Amazing, yeah! Could you two, like, *do* that?"

I looked over at Caroline. She thought about it for a second and then nodded. We could, like, do that.

Chapter 2

A Grand Entrance

The Swift is a 1,200-pound race car. It took six of us to push it backward up the center aisle, which was surprisingly steep. We parked it at the top and blocked both front wheels to stop it from rolling. Caroline and I were given seats up in the last row and told to wait quietly until we were introduced in about two hours. I changed into my red driving suit to match Caroline's red-and-white team uniform. She had become unusually quiet, but the time passed quickly for me. I was fascinated with what the stage crew were doing with cameras, lighting, and direction, which was much more interesting than anything Steve or Brittany had to say. The battering-ram guy and the budgie ladies each had about ten minutes, and I figured that we would get the same. But the news ran long. Finally, they cut to commercials for

at exactly 8:45 a.m. I helped Caroline
 into the Swift. The floor director ran
 and showed her where to steer the car
onto the set, between Steve and Brittany's wicker
chairs.

"Just coast it down and come to a stop in front of
Steve. Piece of cake. You two ready?"

I nodded. Caroline sat and stared blankly at the
stage below.

"OK, I'm heading back down. When I wave, that's
your cue. Just let it roll on down. It'll be fun!"

I looked down at Caroline—artist, photographer,
and—as of this summer—race-team manager.
Normally she was game to take on anything. In her
early twenties, Caroline was very fit, with long
blonde hair, deep blue eyes, and a fashion-model
smile. I'd known her since we were kids; and like her
older brother Rick—my best friend and our race-
team designer—she was energetic, confident, and
fiercely intelligent. But at that moment she did not
look like someone about to have fun. She looked ter-
rified.

"Caroline, are you sure you want to do this?" I
asked. "It's a pretty steep slope."

She kept staring ahead and nodded once. But I
sensed none of her usual confidence. As you can't see

your feet at all when you're sitting in a formula car, I helped Caroline find the brake pedal with her right foot. Then I removed the blocks from the front of the car, grabbed my helmet, and took up a position behind the rear wing. We were ready for the grand entrance.

They came back from commercial. Steve beamed into the camera and nailed our introduction.

"OK, to wrap up the morning, we've got a special treat. I think I feel the need…the need for speed! Am I right, Brittany?"

"Steve, you are so right! Me, too! I've got, like, goose bumps already!"

"All right! Joining us live in the studio is the hottest young driver on the Formula Pacific circuit today, and his team manager. They'll be ripping it up down at Exhibition Place this weekend. So come on, Toronto, let's hear it for…Teddy Stewart and Evelyn Grant!"

A red neon Applause sign lit up, a spotlight swung onto the car, and the audience responded like trained seals, giving us a loud welcome as they turned in their seats to watch our grand entrance. My plan was to give Caroline a gentle push, just to get her rolling, and then jog behind the car with my helmet under my arm as it glided silently down the aisle. The floor director cued us with a wave, and I nudged the Swift's rear wing.

Nothing.

I pushed again, but still the car wouldn't move an inch. The audience sat in silent anticipation as Steve and Brittany's painted smiles began to crack. The seconds ticked away, but I simply could not budge the car.

"Caroline!" I hissed.

"What?"

"Get your foot off the brake!"

"I thought I did! I'm pushing on something, but I can't even see my feet! How do you drive this thing?"

"Just pull your knees up! Don't touch anything with your feet!"

I pushed, Caroline squirmed, but the Swift still refused to move. Finally, I put my helmet down, planted my feet, and really put my shoulder into it. For a few seconds the car remained stuck, and then four things happened at once. Caroline twisted inside the cockpit, the brakes suddenly released, the car shot forward, and I fell flat on my face. I looked up and watched helplessly as the Swift accelerated down the aisle, picking up alarming speed as it headed straight for our smiling hosts. I couldn't see Caroline, but I knew that she was frozen behind the wheel. Brittany reacted first and sprang to the side to avoid the oncoming car. Steve wasn't as quick. He just stood there like a fence post as Caroline and 1,200 pounds of race car bore straight down on him.

Chapter 3

The Teddie & Evelyn Show

There are times when you know in advance that all the laws of physics are going to come together perfectly, so that something rare, and usually bad, will happen. You just know it. When I was a kid growing up in Vancouver, British Columbia, I knew from the crack of the club and the vibration in my palms that the golf ball I had just driven out of our backyard was going to knock the neighbors' cat off their deck and into the fishpond. And it did. Last Thanksgiving, I just knew as soon as I flicked that piece of creamed corn off the side of my dinner plate that it was going to go straight up Rick Grant's nose. And it did.

This was another one of those moments. There was no point in yelling at Caroline to find the brake pedal. No point in chasing after the runaway car. It was simply too late. A rare, bad thing was going to happen. I knew that

Caroline was going to run over Steve with our race car on live TV.

And she did.

The Swift caught Steve just above the ankles with its left front wheel. He went down hard, flat on his back, as the wheel climbed up his legs and past his waist. The car finally came to a stop with the tire resting on his chest. He tried to squirm free by pushing it backward; but by that time Caroline had finally found the brake pedal again, and the car wouldn't move. Steve was pinned and gasping. I ran down the aisle and joined two cameramen. We lifted the front of the car up, and Steve slid out from underneath. He sprang to his feet to wild applause, cleared his throat, snapped his suit jacket straight, checked his hair, and flashed a wide grin. I think everyone in the audience figured we'd planned the whole thing. Caroline sat stunned and motionless in the car, her face the color of cold oatmeal under the bright studio lights.

"Whoa, Teddy, this is one fast car!" Steve gasped.

"And it's such a cool shade of red. Totally!" Brittany gushed.

"Yes, Steve, it's fast," I replied. "And it's Eddie. Eddie Stewart. The paint work was designed by Caroline here, behind the wheel. Caroline Grant."

I didn't want to embarrass the guy any further after

flattening him, but it was important to get the names right. Steve flashed a toothy grin as we stood behind the rear wing of the car and faced the camera.

"Now, let's see how our driver's doing in there, Brittany."

I helped the cameramen turn the car around so that it faced the audience. Brittany kneeled down next to the Swift's cockpit so that she could talk with Caroline, who was staring blankly straight into the camera. She looked like a doe caught in the headlights of a gravel truck.

"OK, Steve. Here I am with DynaSport team manager Caroline Grant. Isn't it, like, totally amazing to have, you know, a woman as a race-team manager?"

Caroline stared straight ahead, unblinking, and slowly said, "Yes…amazing."

Steve jumped in.

"Let's just pull up our chairs and talk speed! Now, Eddie, tell us about this bad boy."

"Well, the car is called a Swift. It's a Formula Atlantic design, handmade in California. It has a Cosworth twin-cam racing engine that makes about 300 horsepower, and a five-speed gearbox. From a standstill, it will reach sixty in about three seconds. On the Exhibition Place street course this weekend we'll top out around 160."

Steve furrowed his brow in concentration, listening intently and nodding in understanding as I spoke.

Then he turned and looked me straight in the eye. It was time for serious race car questions.

"Now, I'm wondering…just how fast will this car go?"

I paused for a moment, wondering if English was Steve's second language.

"It will go 160, Steve."

"Man! 160? Miles per hour?"

"Yes. Miles per hour."

Steve was impressed. "Wow! That's like—"

"That's 256 kilometers per hour!" Brittany interrupted. The camera panned across the car with Caroline, the wax model, frozen in the seat.

"So, Eddie, how many, like, gears does it have?" she asked.

"Five, Brittany. And one in reverse."

"Cool! Just like your Beamer, Steve!"

Steve, the BMW expert, nodded.

"Yes, and you know, Britt, technically that's what racers call a five-speed gearbox."

Steve made quotation marks in the air with his fingers as he said "five-speed gearbox," so there would be no doubt that this was major engineering talk. He pointed to the engine cover.

"Now, what's under the hood of number 28, here?" Steve asked.

We'd been "here" before—about fifteen seconds ago.

At least I had.

"It's a Cosworth twin-cam racing engine. It makes about 300 horsepower," I repeated.

"Whoa, 300 horses! I'll bet that would get you up to sixty pretty fast!"

"In about three seconds, Steve," I said flatly.

Over to Brittany.

"So, Eddie, where do you drive it? To the mall? Like, no way!"

"No, not to the mall. We race it in the North American Formula Atlantic series at tracks across the States and Canada. We'll be racing downtown at Exhibition Place. Here in Toronto. This weekend," I said slowly and clearly.

Steve had received a hand signal from the floor director, which I caught out of the corner of my eye. Time was short, and he wanted Steve to wrap it up quickly.

"All right! Exhibition Place this weekend. I'm there, baby! We're out of time, but I want to thank Teddy and Evelyn from the BynaMow Racing Team, for joining us this morning. Go get 'em, you two! So, until tomorrow, I'm Steve…"

Brittany leaned into the shot.

"And I'm Brittany!"

I barely resisted the temptation to lean in and say, *And I'm not Teddy!*

"And we'll see you tomorrow on 'Wakeup Toronto!' Bye-bye now!" Brittany closed.

Steve and Brittany grinned and waved as the theme music came up, and the audience applauded wildly. I put on a crooked smile while Caroline sat rock-solid in the car, a blonde statue in the glare of the set lights.

"And we're clear!" yelled the floor director as the set lights dimmed.

I stood up, helped Caroline out, and sat her down. One of the studio crew brought her a glass of water. She was slowly coming around as Steve rushed off, but Brittany unclipped her mike and sat down next to us.

"Thanks, you two. That was great. Caroline will be fine in a few minutes, I expect. Stage fright is not uncommon in amateurs. The lights and the cameras can tend to promote rapid cognitive overload, resulting in a temporary, although quite harmless, state of disorientation."

What? Who was this? Brittany's brilliant twin sister?

"One last question, Eddie. Going over my research earlier this morning, I noticed that the Formula Atlantic series has produced drivers like Jacques Villeneuve, who have gone on to win the Indy 500 and the Formula One world championship. See that in your future?" she asked.

"Well, someday I hope," I replied.

Brittany smiled and got up to leave. But as she caught

the expression of disbelief on my face, she paused. And then she read my mind.

"Don't believe everything you see on TV. People aren't always what they seem. Better to stick with reality. And good luck on Sunday."

Chapter 4

Miss Math

Caroline came out of her daze in about ten minutes. She even managed to see the bizarre side of running down poor Steve. We loaded the Swift back into the trailer, and by midmorning we had returned to our pit area in downtown Toronto. A large banner greeted us as we pulled in. In red letters inside a border of small hearts, someone had printed, "Welcome Home, Teddy & Evelyn!"

We climbed out of the truck, and I just had to shake my head and laugh. The morning TV show must have been something to see. Standing proudly under the banner, wearing her trademark XL Hawaiian floral dress and her huge straw and wax-fruit hat, was Sophia Novello, ex–Italian restaurant owner, currently owner of our race team, and my wild aunt. Sophie was a short and rather large middle-aged lady with energy to burn and a heart of gold. *And* fearless taste in clothes.

"Eddie! Caroline! You two were marvelous!" Sophie chirped.

"You watched it?" I asked stupidly.

"I taped it! It was very nice, I think. Very cute. Come inside and see."

Before we could walk over to Sophie's huge motor home, Rick Grant, our race engineer and Caroline's brother, shuffled up stiffly, as if in a trance. His mouth hung open, and his glazed eyes were wide as he stared vacantly into the distance. In exactly the same dead, monotone voice Caroline had used in the TV interview, he said, "Yes...amazing."

I couldn't help cracking up at Rick's perfect impersonation, but all it got him from Caroline was a swift slug in the shoulder. She gave me a frosty glare, tossed her head, and said, "Very mature, boys. Unload the car, and then you'd better check into the hotel. Some of us have work to do." And with that, she walked briskly into the motor home and closed the door firmly behind her.

Actually, it was amazing that we were still racing in Formula Atlantic at all. Our team had started the summer racing a homebuilt Trans-Am Mustang and hoping for a break. We got one after pulling a fellow driver from a wreck. He offered us the chance to race his damaged Formula Atlantic car, if we could repair it in time for the race in Milwaukee. With the help of Allan Tanner, a first-class British race engineer, we managed to get the damaged car back together, took it to the Milwaukee Oval, and finished second by a car length. That got the attention of Mr. John R. Reynolds, president of DynaSport Industries, who offered to sponsor our team for the rest of the season.

Caroline had booked us into a great old hotel right in the heart of Toronto's downtown, in the Exhibition Place area, where once a year the city streets were closed off to form a race course. I usually roomed with Rick, Caroline's older brother, professional engineer, race car designer, one of my lifelong best friends, and easily the smartest guy I'd ever met.

We found our room, and unpacked. Then I went out for a run while Rick powered up one of his laptops and got to work on suspension settings for the race. I found a great running path along Lake Ontario's shoreline and stayed on it for a good five miles, out and back. After the long haul from the last race in Milwaukee, Wisconsin, it felt great to be active, out from behind the wheel of the tow truck, and getting ready to race again in a few days.

After a long shower, I took everyone out for pizza

(OK, so I'm cheap). Over coffee and dessert, Rick grabbed the sports section of a local newspaper from a vacant table and found an article on the previous race in Milwaukee, where I'd finished second. The headline read, *Rookie Driver Turns Heads in First Race*.

Using his excellent Elvis impersonation, Rick began reading the article aloud until Caroline snatched the paper away from him and scanned the official results summary at the end. After a few seconds, she sat up straight in her chair, borrowed a pen from Rick, and quickly began writing numbers in the margin.

"Eddie, what are the Formula Atlantic points standings right now?" she asked, checking her figures.

"Who knows?" I mumbled through a mouthful of cheesecake.

Sophie kicked me under the table and glared. "Do not talk with your mouth full."

"Well, maybe you *should* know," Caroline continued. "According to this, you're in the hunt for the series title."

I moved my legs out of Sophie's range and stopped chewing.

"The title? After one race? No way."

She pointed to the article.

"Yes, way. I checked it twice. Listen to this: the article reviews the Atlantic season up to Milwaukee. So far, no one has dominated any of the top three places. It's a short series, just six races, and they award championship points for finishing first through sixth, right? Ten points for a win, eight points for second, six for third, then four, two, and one point for sixth place. So, before our team came together, Stefan Veilleux won the first race in Phoenix, Arizona; Kurt Heinrich was nowhere; and Raul DaSilva didn't even finish. Then, Raul won the next two races in California, at Long Beach and at Laguna Seca. Heinrich picked up a few points, but Veilleux got none. Heinrich then won in Milwaukee; you, Mr. Pizza Boy, were second, and Veilleux was third. Raul got no points there, and a whole bunch of different guys have finished fourth, fifth or sixth in each of those first four races. Bottom line, it's still wide open for the title with two more races to go—Toronto, this weekend, and the final in Miami."

"Thank you, Miss Math," Rick replied. "And all of this means what for us, exactly?"

"It means that if you read more than the comics in the newspaper, Richard, you would know that Raul DaSilva has a very slim lead. He's only two points up on his teammate, Kurt Heinrich, and four up on

Stefan Veilleux. That's it. And guess who is sitting fourth in the championship right now? Fast Eddie Stewart."

This time everyone stopped eating.

Chapter 5

Possibilities

Two races. If we won them both, or even finished in the top three, and especially if the other top three drivers failed to score, well then....

Nah. Impossible. Or was it?

We were all thinking it, but no one wanted to say it—except Herb MacDonald, our crew chief and my other lifelong best friend. If Rick was the smartest guy I'd ever met, Herb was easily the strongest. He came through the door at 6 feet, 4 inches and 240 pounds. With his jet-black hair and heavy, dark glasses, he looked exactly like Clark Kent, Superman's human double. We called him the Man of Steel.

"It could happen, you guys," Herb stated calmly. "We could win this thing."

He said this as a statement of fact, as if he were

merely announcing that it would snow tomorrow. In August.

"When was the last time I was wrong, Eddie?" he asked.

"At 10:00 a.m., August tenth, grade seven summer camp at Lake Cowichan," I replied instantly. We'd had this discussion before. Many times.

"No, you always get that backward," he snapped back. "I only thought I was wrong, but in the end I was right. You always forget that—"

Sophie cut us off.

"Shush! It is not important now, Herbie. You and Eddie can argue later." She turned to our race engineer, Allan Tanner.

"Mr. Tanner, what do you think? Is there a chance?"

Allan Tanner took a long sip of his coffee, stroked his short beard, and looked at the expectant eyes around the table. Allan was British and in his late thirties; he had joined our team as race engineer just before Milwaukee. His racing background spanned twenty years, and he had worked on everything from karts to Formula One cars. We had managed to talk him into helping us on a race-to-race basis after he quit Raul DaSilva's team. Allan spoke quietly, with the authority of someone who had guided teams to championships before.

"Mathematically, yes, the possibility exists. But it's a slim one," he said. "Very slim. DaSilva and his teammate Heinrich have an enormous budget. They have the best of everything—and they're ruthless. Believe me, I know. Raul will do whatever it takes to win the title, and never mind the rules. So those two are likely to finish near the front in the next two races. The Frenchman, Stefan Veilleux, runs hot and cold, but he can be very fast. And need I remind all of you that our experience as a team totals exactly one race? We did well at Milwaukee—very well, actually. But one race certainly does not make a championship."

Sophie was disappointed. "So then there is no hope?"

"No, by all means have hope; have faith. Just be realistic and take it one step at a time. Look after what we can control; focus on that and let the rest take care of itself. We can't control what other teams choose to do, what parts of the car may fail, or what the track conditions may be. There are so many things in this business that can change instantly, so many variables, that only a fool thinks he's got it all worked out in advance. So, yes, we have reason to be optimistic. Let's expect to do well, but at the same time, remember, this isn't Hollywood."

True enough, but I still had to give my head a shake.

Our fortunes as a race team had improved literally overnight. At the start of the summer, we were three guys with a home-built Mustang, no sponsor, no prospects beyond the next race, and a distant dream of someday moving up in professional formula racing. Now, by midsummer, I was driving a Formula Atlantic car, working with a top race engineer, and backed up by my buddies, a major corporate sponsor, a manager, and a chef. We even had a motor home.

"You're right, it's not Hollywood," Herb agreed. "It's downtown Toronto. And I say we've got as good a shot as anyone."

On that point, I had to agree with The Man of Steel. Judging by the last few months, anything was possible. Maybe even a run for the title.

Chapter 6

Driving Tips with Stefan

I got my first look at the Toronto street circuit the next morning. As usual we were in town with the Trans-Am teams. We were part of the weekend show leading up to the featured Champ Car race on Sunday afternoon. Drawing more than 150,000 people, over three days, this race weekend was the biggest spectator event of the year in Toronto, maybe even in Canada. The organizers had laid on a tour for the drivers. On Thursday morning, we were driven slowly around the track in golf carts, stopping to inspect each corner. The golf carts were nothing like a race car, but at least I found out where to turn left and right.

The two-mile-long Toronto course used regular city streets and was wide and flat. There were eleven turns—all but four to the right—and two long straights, both ending in sharp ninety-degree corners.

It was obviously a track that would be hard on brakes and gearboxes. The downforce from the wings would have to be balanced against speed on the straights. If we set the wings for lots of downforce, the car would be fast through the corners; but we would pay for it with increased drag on the straights, where the wing would reduce the top speed. On the other hand, if we went for a setup with minimum drag and low downforce, we would be rocket-fast down the straights, but slow through the corners. As ever, the trick would be to find the right balance.

Someone who knew a few tricks around here was also one of the top drivers in the Atlantic series, Stefan Veilleux, from France. At maybe 5 feet, 5 inches, with a mass of curly black hair, twinkling brown eyes, and a mischievous grin, you couldn't help but like Stefan. Although he looked like a hobbit, he was a racer. He had run at Toronto last year, and he offered to draw me a map over coffee in his motor home. I paid close attention for two reasons. First, this was a tough track, and second, Stefan's rapid-fire, broken English often left me in the dark.

"This circuit, she is hard to driving for you, Eedie Stewart. She is, how do you say…a moose!"

"A moose?"

He'd lost me already. Stefan frowned and searched for the words.

"Ah, how is it? You know…she is big…mean …dangerous!" He made claws out of his hands, and bared his teeth. It wasn't a moose—a crazed chipmunk, maybe, but never a moose. It was like playing charades.

"Wait! A bear? You mean it's a bear of a track?"

"*Oui!* Yes, Eedie, she is the bear! A big, black, grizzled bear."

Stefan grabbed a piece of paper and began to draw a map of the track.

"So, Eedie Stewart, here you are in your fast red racing car. You crosses the start/finish line in the fifth gear. Very fast here. Then, you brakes hard for turn one. You turns in easy and nice to the right, shifts down to the first gear, then you are to push hard! Up to the third gear through turn two, and then the big, long, straight road—very fast, flat-out!"

"Right. Thunder Alley." On the city map it was actually Lakeshore Boulevard, which sounds very calm and peaceful. On race weekend, it became Thunder Alley, home to packs of shrieking Formula cars racing wheel to wheel, at three times the normal speed limit.

"*Oui*, yes, the big road. OK, so now, Eedie, he is

going under a little people's bridge, *zoom*, then he brake very hard for turn three. The first gear now. He watch for the pass here because Eedie knows that it is the best place. Everyone want to pass here. Now he go through the turn three, and it is…it is…the snake."

"A snake?"

Stefan was stuck again. He put his hands up, side-by-side, and moved them together. More charades.

"Thin? No. Wait…narrow? The road gets narrow?" I asked.

"*Oui*, yes! Narrow. OK. Only one car is having the space. Any more cars, and it is bang, squish, good-bye! Then, Eedie, it is a little flick left for turn four, then down to the second gear for turn five."

He had dropped the pencil and was moving his hands and feet now, as he mentally drove the course. He even did all the sound effects. I retrieved the pencil and made notes furiously.

"Turn right, then the third gear!

"Eedie drifts his car like the eagle that soars through turn six, and then the fourth and the fifth gear, very fast now, sweeps through turn seven, *zoom*! But then! The brake! Hard, hard, hard on the brake and quickly the first gear for turn eight! It is a sharp right, and then, yes, a sharp left through turn nine!

"Big fun here!"

Stefan closed his eyes. He was having trouble staying in his chair as he reacted to the imaginary G-forces.

"Now, Eedie Stewart, he accelerates! He pushes hard through turn ten and eleven. They are a snake, but Eedie is he afraid? No, it is to laugh for him! He is a man to lives for the danger! Now he is flat in the fifth gear, *zoom*, he crosses the finish, and then…"

I was almost breathless. "Then…?"

Stefan closed his eyes and nodded slowly. "Then, Eedie Stewart, he knows. He has done it—the lap of perfection!"

Got it. The perfect lap. All I had to do for Saturday afternoon was repeat it twenty-seven times in a row.

Chapter 7

Pet Care

Our first practice session was on Thursday afternoon. Allan wanted me to put maximum track miles on the car, making sure that we had the right gear ratios and a basic suspension and wing setup. Any setup changes would come tonight and tomorrow, before qualifying. I also needed seat time to learn the track and to see if Stefan's advice really helped me know where to go hard and where to be careful.

We did about thirty laps in the forty-five-minute session, and the car ran perfectly. At first I felt trapped in between the tall office buildings, concrete barriers, and steel-mesh catch fences that lined every inch of the circuit. There was none of the open space of a true road course, or even of the grass borders on the inside of turns, which ovals have. As I expected, the Toronto track was like blasting around inside a concrete tunnel, with absolutely no room for mistakes. Still, it was a major rush to hammer around in a formula car, flat-out on city streets, with bursts of acceleration followed by hard braking and very precise entry lines into each corner. This was definitely a track that would be hard on machinery—and on brains. Lose concentration for a second or two at this place, and I knew that I'd find a wall or a catch fence, faster than I could blink. A decent Formula Atlantic lap time for Toronto was in the 1:10 minute range. Toward the end of the session, I was putting up consistent and comfortable times of 1:09, confirming that we had a good basic setup.

As I pulled in and climbed out, Herb was waiting. I'd known Herb since we were kids at summer camp, and he had two great passions in his life. One was food—especially pancakes—and the other was looking after things. Herb's sheer size and strength often intimidated people, but inside that massive frame was a calm and gentle heart. I learned that the summer I met Bob. Most guys grew up with pets to look after, but Herb had terrible allergies as a kid, so he could never have anything furry like a cat, a dog, or a hamster. So instead, he had to make do with something else. He chose a plant— actually, a small brown cactus. He named it Bob.

Herb brought Bob along to youth camp every August. He took him for walks, and even taught him tricks. Bob was able to sit, stay, and was especially good at playing dead. No one ever dared to ask any questions. When Bob finally expired, Herb turned his affections to machines. He became a master mechanic and machinist, and he had built race cars for me since I started racing. So I understood completely when his relationship with our new Formula Atlantic car went beyond just working on it. Herb didn't just work on it. He watched it on the track, listened to it, and talked to it quietly. The Swift wasn't just another race car. It was his latest pet, and he looked after it.

I went to the motor home, got out of my driving suit, and returned to find that Herb had raised the Swift onto work stands and was stripping the front suspension. This wasn't fine tuning. It was major.

"What's the problem?" I asked.

"This," he replied, running his hand over a weld, where two lengths of steel tubing joined to support the top of the right front wheel. It looked fine to me.

"It's stressed too much at this joint. You're really standing on the brakes here, Eddie, and it's flexing, deflecting, and from there it may even break. Can't see it yet, but it will get worse as the race goes on. This is not a happy race car."

Thinking back, I had noticed that the front of the car was darting around under hard braking. I had just put it down to the bumps in the track surface, but Herb knew better. It would be vital to have a race setup that made sure I could pull the car down, straight and true, from 160 mph to 30 in about three seconds at the end of Thunder Alley—and the last thing I needed was a suspension failure.

"Actually, it was starting to dart around a bit, braking for turn three," I confirmed.

"Sure it was. I know what this puppy wants," he beamed.

It was time for pet care. I left Herb humming, and went over the practice times with Allan and Rick. They were basically satisfied that we would be competitive for qualifying tomorrow. Then, out of the blue, Rick grabbed a torque wrench and used it as a microphone. Aside from race-car design, he also did great impersonations, and his favorite was Elvis. Rick easily slid into a slow Memphis drawl as he became Elvis, the TV motor-sports announcer.

"Well, thankya...thankya very much. I'm here in Toronto, Canada, with Fast Eddie Stewart, hottest racer on the Formula Atlantic circuit. Mercy, he's just a hunka drivin' love! And joinin' us is his race engineer, Allan Tanner. So, come on, boys, tell me now.

Tell me what it's like out there."

Allan and I just stared blankly at each other. We were new to improvised comedy.

"The boys seem to be stuck for an answer just now. Why? 'Cause they just don't know what it's like out there. But soon...yeah, real soon...they're gonna know."

I looked across at Allan again, but he just shrugged.

"Listen to me now! Don't want no more embarrassing moments on live TV for young Eddie. No, sir! 'Cause now he's got himself the new Grant Race Data System! It ain't available in stores; it's only $49.95, and if ya order right now, I'll even throw in a pair of flameproof socks worn by Eddie himself in Milwaukee! Yeah! So, pick up that phone and call me now! Operators are standin' by to—"

I snapped my hand over Rick's mouth.

"Sold. I'll take one. And give Elvis a rest. Now what is the Grant Race Data System?"

Chapter 8

The Data King

Rick dashed into the motor home and returned with a thick file filled with drawings and pages of charts, calculations, and printouts. He spread the pages out across the steel work table. Allan recognized what was in front of him.

"Full onboard data acquisition," he said with admiration. "Standard in Formula One and Champ Car these days, but quite rare at this level. And very pricey. Buying a system like this would be expensive."

"Buy?" Rick looked mildly insulted. "With enough money, anyone could go out and buy a system like this. No challenge to that. I want to build one."

Allan smiled. "I thought you might."

"What exactly does this do, Allan?" I asked.

"It's based upon aerospace technology. Data

acquisition is an electronic system in which an aircraft, spacecraft, or ground vehicle is completely wired with dozens of very small and very precise sensors. In a racing car, the sensors can measure every movement of dozens of parts of the car. It takes measurements hundreds of times per second, and the sensors are precise to fractions of a millimeter. A small onboard computer in the nose section stores the information, which can then be downloaded to a laptop when the car returns to the pits. For example, say the car feels unstable to you in a high-speed left turn, but it's fine in a similar turn to the right. What would you do, Edward?"

"Bring it in and adjust the suspension," I replied.

"Right, but the trick is know what to adjust and by how much. You might try camber, toe-in or spring rates—maybe all three. You change something, go out and see if it's better. If not, you come in, try something else, go out, come in again, and on it goes. One thing at a time. At best it's educated guesswork. It can take hours, even days to find the right setup."

"Which is where these little hummers come in," Rick said. "Once I place and wire these sensors, we'll be able to build a detailed database of what the car's doing, and how you're driving it, every second, under braking, acceleration, through every turn, and over every bump on this track. I mean, you sneeze in the car, and we'll know it, Eddie. I can import the data into my software model, make changes to the setup, and see the results almost instantly on the laptop. Then we fine-tune the car and send you right back out with a great setup. I could even run a simulation of the entire race."

Incredible. If it worked, we could have the answers we needed in minutes rather than in hours of experimenting. While other teams would be in and out of the pits searching for the best setup, I could put in a few hot laps, come in, and upload the information to Rick's laptop. He would then run his simulation program, compute the best setup, Herb would make the mechanical adjustments, and I'd be out again in minutes with a race car perfectly adjusted for the track and weather conditions. We already had the best rear-wing design in the series, thanks to Rick, and it looked like he was going to give us another advantage. He gathered his design drawings, placed them back into the file, and grinned like he'd just won first place in the National Science Fair. Again.

"Well done, Rick," Allan smiled. "Very well done, indeed. Only two problems though—money and time."

Rick had worked that out, too. "I called around and

found that I can get everything I need locally. I'll have it installed by midnight, tops."

That meant at least noon tomorrow. Rick's sense of time was often in another dimension.

"And the cost?" Allan asked.

Rick thumbed through his papers until he found the one he wanted.

"You're right, it's not cheap. For everything, about $18,000—say twenty grand at the outside."

I looked at Allan, and he nodded. We could do it. Thank you, DynaSport Industries, our new corporate sponsor.

Chapter 9

Front Row

As I predicted, it did take Rick all night, and until noon the next day, to install his data logging system on the Swift. Herb stayed up to help him. I arrived from the hotel, well rested, and found Rick sitting in the car with his laptop as Herb was completing the final adjustments.

"Eddie! Excellent! This is so cool! I just tested it; it's great; it's fabulous—here, look!"

Herb looked fairly normal for having been up all night. He was good at it. But I was worried about Rick. He was talking so fast that I thought he was going to sprain his tongue. I knelt down beside the car and looked hard into Rick's swollen, bloodshot eyes. Then I frowned at Herb.

"Herb, you let him have *real* coffee, didn't you?"

Most people made regular coffee, but regular

wasn't even close to being strong enough for Herb. He bought custom-roasted beans, ground them by hand, and used a coffee machine custom made in Switzerland to make what he called real coffee. It was a thick, rich, jet-black brew, with enough caffeine to double your heart rate just by smelling it. And I knew that Rick had been drinking it all night. Herb held up his hands in defense.

"Hey, look, Eddie, I tried to tell him. 'Rick,' I said, 'You're not used to it. Go easy.' But you know Rick. Would he listen? No."

I returned my gaze to Rick, whose wide eyes were darting like lasers from instrument to instrument on the Swift's dashboard.

"Hey, Eddie, listen. What if I built you a small data display and I can put one right here and you could monitor performance as you're driving and right from inside the car during the race and everything and then we could talk on the radio and stuff and I'd be able to make the changes like that and so, what do you think?"

"I think you need to lie down, Rick. Come on. Out."

Rick protested, but Herb and I dragged him out of the car and locked him in the back bedroom of the motor home. We gave Sophie strict instructions that he was grounded until we had to report for the qual-ifying round.

An express courier had arrived that morning with boxes from DynaSport's head office. They contained a supply of decals, crests, hats, jackets, golf tees, key chains, pens, and just about anything else you could think of that could carry the imprint of their corporate name. The red Swift now had our new sponsor's logo across both front and rear wings and on both side pods. Crests had been sewn onto crew uniforms and my driving suits, and Caroline advised us that for the rest of the season we were officially DynaSport Motorsports. It looked great, and our image with the other Atlantic teams improved immediately. We had Rick's original rear-wing design, which almost won us the last race, we were fast enough to sit fourth in the championship, and now we had attracted a major corporate sponsor. We were no longer the new guys. We had arrived.

There was a lunch break, a brief drivers' meeting, and then a thirty-minute warm-up for the Atlantic cars. Herb wanted to see if the front suspension was better, and Rick needed me to put in as many laps as possible to collect data for him to analyze. I ran for the full thirty minutes, easily lapping at race speed in the 1:10 range, practicing my brake points and cornering lines. As usual, Herb was right. The Swift felt much more stable than yesterday, under hard braking and over the bumps. And we had set Rick's rear wing for a nice balance between downforce and straight-line speed.

When the warm-up was over, I came in, and Rick plugged a cable into a small socket in the nose of the Swift. Then he uploaded the data to his laptop and got busy analyzing it. We had an hour until qualifying, and the car felt ready. I didn't think that we needed to change much of anything, but the computer model revealed a couple of areas where we could improve.

The guys made the fine tuning adjustments based upon Rick's analysis, while Sophie, Caroline, and I met with the owners of DynaSport. John Reynolds (he insisted we call him J.R.) and his wife, Susan, had arrived in their Ferrari to see their new team in action. We gave them a tour of the pit, explained the basics of the race car, and reviewed the competition. They were fascinated. Caroline and J.R. discovered that they had a shared interest in photography, and Susan had a long discussion with Sophie about pasta sauces that ended with an exchange of original recipes. And I thought we were just here to race cars.

Qualifying began in the mid-afternoon. There were

two groups of cars, fast and slow, based upon their performance at the last race. As we had finished second in the previous race in Milwaukee, we went out with the fast guys. That felt good. I knew Allan's approach; I put in the usual five laps to warm everything up, pitted to check tires and wings, and then did ten more hard laps to set a fast qualifying time. As Stefan had explained, the Toronto course was so tight and narrow that there were really only two good spots to pass, so it would be critical to qualify well here. If I got stuck back in the middle of the pack it would take a very long time to work up to the front. Better to start up there.

Even with this fast group, I knew that we were flying. The Swift cornered flat and true. We were pulling hard down the straights, and I found that I could brake later and more smoothly than any other driver, especially at the end of Lakeshore Boulevard, the best passing zone. Some guys were locking up and smoking their front tires trying to slow down there. A few out-braked themselves, missed the corner completely, and had to take the escape road. Not us. On every lap, the Swift's nose dipped slightly under heavy braking and turned smoothly into the sharp corners. It allowed me to get on the gas early and improve my exit speed. Herb had been right.

Allan stayed off the radio, allowing me full concentration, but Herb had the pit board out. Each time I passed the pits he put up the last two numbers of each lap time. We started in the one-minute, nine-second range, which he put up as 09. Soon I started to see 82, then 76, and finally a 75.

We got the checkered flag to end the session, and I had to know. I hit the small radio button on the steering wheel on the way back to the pits.

"Allan. Talk to me!"

"Yes, Edward?" he replied calmly.

"Where are we? I saw a 1:07 on the board."

"Actually 1:0755. You're front row, next to Veilleux, on the pole."

Yes! A front-row start was ideal, the car was fast, and Stefan was a guy I was comfortable running flat-out with.

Perfect.

Then it started to rain.

Chapter 10

Darkening Skies

I t started with a few large raindrops on my helmet visor as I cruised back to our pit. By the time I had unbuckled and climbed out of the Swift, the sky had turned angry, with massive black clouds churning everywhere. A fierce wind drove the rain down in cold, hard sheets, and everyone ran to find some shelter. All, except the poor Trans-Am drivers who were just starting their qualifying session. They would have to do it in a rainstorm. We sprinted for the safety of Sophie's huge motor home.

Given the choice of racing in the rain and having both front teeth drilled clean through without any freezing, most race drivers would go for the dental work. Not all, but most. Driving a normal road car in heavy rain is bad enough, but at least you're dry and can keep the windshield clear with the wipers and defrosters. Driving an open-wheeled Formula Atlantic car in a downpour, around a wet racetrack, is worse—a lot worse. First, you sit in an open cockpit with no windshield, which guarantees that you will be instantly and thoroughly soaked. You are basically a sponge with a helmet. Second, you have to squint ahead through your helmet visor, which has no wiper to keep it clear, often fogs up, and is always covered with wet spray. Third, in the rain you have a lot less grip, so the car is a handful every second. And worst of all, open-wheeled race cars have no fenders, so at almost any speed they throw huge rooster tails of spray high into the air. If you are unfortunate enough to be behind another car, you're driving almost blind at-one-hundred-plus miles per hour.

Allan rubbed a clear spot on the misty kitchen window of the motor home and peered out.

"If this keeps up, I'm going to get homesick for England."

J.R. joined him.

"The weather forecast says we're in for rain until tomorrow night," he said, squinting out through the window. "Too bad. Rained out at our first race."

Herb had made about five gallons of real coffee, and he was passing around steaming mugs to everyone. We all crammed into the kitchen, listened to the rain hammer on the roof, and watched the windows fog up. He passed a mug to J.R.

"Rained out?" Herb replied. "Never. Maybe in baseball. Not in this game. We go rain, shine, sleet, snow, whatever."

J.R.'s first sip of Herb's brew actually brought tears to his eyes. He blinked and cleared his throat. I smiled quietly to myself.

"Wow, Herb! This tastes...uh...incredible. Anyway, you're not serious. You're not really going to go out and try to race in these conditions."

Herb looked amazed, as if someone wanted to call off the Super Bowl because it was getting dark.

"Sure, we will. We just set up the car for rain, that's all. 'Racing in the wet,' Allan calls it. We run soft, sticky rain tires with deep grooves. We set up the suspension on the car so it rolls lazily into the corners, and we crank up the angle on the wings to get as much downforce as possible. The driver has to have soft hands, to feel every twitch in the wheel. And he needs to do everything very smoothly, very gently. It's a real balancing act to go fast in the rain, and not many guys can do it. Eddie can. When we ran Formula Ford a few years back, he just about lapped the field in a monsoon at Portland. So, yeah, we'll run in this. No sweat."

Growing up in the Pacific Northwest, I was used to rain. In fact, Vancouver is inside a rain forest, and I always said that the province of British Columbia's official flower was mildew. I had raced and won in "the wet" quite a few times, and I remembered that Portland race in the old Van Dieman well. Once I got out of the spray of the other cars and got used to sliding around, it was like racing on snow or loose gravel, hanging the tail out and controlling long, drifting slides. I thought it was great fun—a lot like downhill ski racing or snowboarding. For me, anyway, rain wasn't a problem.

But we did have a setup problem. We had tuned the Swift perfectly for a dry track and slick tires based on Rick's data system. But we had zero data for a wet track and rain tires. We were back to a best-guess setup, but then again, so was everyone else. We still had the advantage of Rick's rear wing, and Allan's setup knowledge. The huge bonus was that, starting on the front row, I wouldn't have any spray coming at me. Unless Stefan beat me to the first corner. I felt sorry for anyone starting midfield or farther back. Those guys would be accelerating hard into a fire hose.

The Trans-Am cars got through a crash-filled qualifying session with the rain pounding down even harder than before. The constant racket on the motor home's roof began to make conversation difficult, and the pit area was rapidly turning into a new part of Lake Ontario. The decision was made quickly. We would lock everything up, retreat to the hotel, and see what the weather was like tomorrow. If it cleared up and was dry, then the Swift was ready. If it was still raining, then we would have lots of time to change the setup.

John and Susan Reynolds insisted on buying us dinner, which they did at a small Greek place. J.R. ate almost as much as Herb. Then he announced that the DynaSport Toronto office had a corporate box at the SkyDome. The Toronto Argonauts were playing the Montreal Alouettes that night. J.R. absolutely loved Canadian football, and it would be a great place to get out of the rain. So we all took in the game. Herb and I enjoy football, and both of us had played some in high school. I was a wide receiver—that's where "Fast Eddie" originally came from—and Herb had been a ferocious defensive end. As a former All-American linebacker, J.R. expertly analyzed the entire first half for Sophie and Allan, who had never seen a North American football game. Allan observed that the game would be almost as tough as English rugby, if they took the players' pads and helmets away. But

Sophie didn't understand why the players slapped each other on their bums after a good play. Susan Reynolds then launched into a detailed explanation of football as a primitive caveman type of bonding ritual that involved muscular men in tight pants. The girls found this hilarious. Herb and John took up the argument, and I tried to convince them of the elegance of the Fire-Offense strategy, but we got nowhere. By the third quarter, the Argos were up by twenty-four points, so it was a good time for me to say goodnight, grab a cab back to the hotel, and turn in early.

The rain let up slightly through the night, but when I pulled back the curtains at 6:00 the next morning, the sky remained low and slate gray. I flicked on the weather channel and confirmed that we would be in for a wet race. I don't know what time Rick got back to our room, but it must have been late. He was snoring peacefully, so I left him a note saying I'd gone to the track. I grabbed my gear, drank a coffee, hailed a cab, and made it back to our pit area at first light by 6:30.

I splashed through the drizzle and puddles, found my set of keys, and got ready to unlock the door of the motor home. I didn't have to. It swung wide open as soon as I touched the handle.

Chapter 11

Motive and Opportunity

I wondered if, in last night's rush, someone had forgotten to lock up. I stepped inside, turned on the lights, and knew something was different—not wrong exactly, but it just felt different. There were no obvious signs of a break-in, and no one had trashed the place. Everything was neat and where it should have been. Then I noticed the footprints in the carpeting. They were still wet. Someone had been in here, and recently. I checked the cupboard where Sophie kept some cash inside an old cereal box. It was all there. Caroline had thousands of dollars' worth of camera and video equipment in the back bedroom, along with two of Rick's laptops and the DVD system. All of it was still there. Everything worth stealing was left untouched.

I carefully inspected every cupboard, drawer, and box in that motor home. Everything was there, but some of Rick's papers and files had been gone through and were scattered across the small desk. I went outside and checked the door, which, upon closer inspection, showed signs of having been forced open. I got out my keys again and went to the side door of our thirty-five-foot aluminum trailer. It was also wide open.

I knew then that something was definitely wrong. Herb would never leave the trailer containing his tools—and especially his race car—unless everything was locked securely. I flicked on the overhead lights and knelt close to the floor. Again I found the wet outlines of footprints, two sets this time. My worst nightmare would have been to find that someone had stolen the car and our equipment, but the red Swift sat there silently along with all of our wheels, tools, and pit equipment. Still, something was out of place. Crouching low, I tracked the footprints slowly along the steel floor toward the back of the trailer where I found some wrenches by the rear wheel. Then, right near the double rear door, I slowly looked up—and had my answer. The car was still here, at least most of it. The entire rear wing was gone. I quickly glanced up to the ceiling of the trailer where we kept the original factory wing as a spare. Also gone.

I leaned back heavily against the Swift's rear tire,

listened to the rain drumming on the roof, and tried to put it together. Someone breaks into the motor home, walks past stuff worth thousands of dollars, but takes nothing. Some papers are gone through. Looking for what? Then the intruder is joined by an assistant. They break into the trailer, grab some tools, remove the rear wing from our car, take the spare wing as well, and just walk out the back door of the trailer and disappear into the rain. Without a rear wing, we would not be racing today. I pushed the double rear doors with my foot to test my theory, watched them slowly swing open, and stared blankly as fresh drops began to spatter on the floor of the trailer.

For some reason, a detective novel that I had written a book report on, for Mr. Saunders back in grade eight in Vancouver, drifted into my mind. I couldn't remember the title of the book or the plot, but something the detective had said came back clearly. Motive and opportunity. A criminal always needed both. Motive was a reason to commit a crime, and opportunity was the chance to do it. A simple formula to solve a crime. So, I sat on the floor and played detective. I started with opportunity. Who had a chance to break into our vehicles last night? Any one of thirty Atlantic teams parked around us in the pit area, which narrowed it down to about 400 people. No help there.

What about motive? Why would someone steal two race car wings, instead of tools, computers, and video equipment, which could easily be sold on the street for cash? It had to be someone who wanted to make certain that we couldn't make the race. Who would be prepared to commit theft to make that happen? It took about a nanosecond for one name to surface. Raul DaSilva went straight to the top of my list.

DaSilva was an arrogant, weasel-faced millionaire from Brazil. He had more money than many small countries, and he used it to buy the best equipment and people for his Ascension Motorsports team. Earlier in the season, Raul had employed Allan Tanner as his race engineer, until Allan got fed up and quit. Good for us, bad for Raul. He also drove to win at any cost. I'd seen him deliberately cause an accident with a rookie driver earlier in the season, and we'd had words after I reported him to the race officials. As things were now, Allan was working with us, and Rick had designed a wing for our car that had helped me beat Raul and just about everyone else at the last race in Milwaukee. I was now someone who could catch him for the championship. Our rear wing was an advantage that nobody else had, and I had just used that edge to put our car on the front row and solidly in front of Raul. I knew that I wasn't exactly his favorite guy.

So in my mind, it had to be DaSilva. He had both opportunity and motive. And something else came back too; I remembered what Allan had said to Raul the day he quit, about Raul's complete lack of respect for everything—maybe including the law. Stealing someone else's property wouldn't bother Raul in the least, especially if it put us out and gave him an edge. The more I thought about it, the more it made sense. My shock soon gave way to certainty and then to growing anger. I was close to grabbing a crowbar, storming across the pits to Raul's enormous Ascension Motorsports transporter, forcing the door open, and retrieving the wings, *our* wings, that I was certain were inside. I just might have done it too, if Herb's massive frame hadn't stepped through the open back door at that moment.

"Hey, racer boy, you sleep here last night or what?"

"I wish I had," I replied pointing to the rear of the Swift.

Herb knelt down and carefully let his eyes roam over the car and the floor, inspecting every inch, following the footprints from the side door to his toolbox, back to the rear of the trailer, and up to the ceiling. I let him take it all in, wanting to see if he reached the same conclusion. He did.

"Two guys, Eddie. An hour ago, maybe less. And

they knew what they were doing. They knew exactly which tools to use and which bolts to take out. Probably had the whole rear wing assembly off in two minutes, grabbed the spare, and were out the back door and gone."

I nodded in agreement. I expected Herb to be as shocked, outraged, and angry as I was. Instead, he just quietly shook his head. This wasn't just theft for him, it was personal. Someone had hurt his race car.

"Come on," I said, standing up. "Let's you and I go over and give Raul DaSilva a wake-up call he'll never forget!"

"Why do you think it's DaSilva?" Herb asked.

"I don't think it was him, I know it! His transporter is maybe 200 feet away; he needs us out of the race today to keep his points lead; he thinks he can get away with anything. And he's got it in for me anyway. Who else?"

Herb picked his tools off the floor, went to the front of the trailer, wiped them with a rag, and quietly put them away. He slowly closed the toolbox drawer and stood very still for a few moments.

"If it is him, or his guys, we can't just go over and kick in the door, Eddie."

"Yeah? Just watch me."

Herb smiled. Although he could likely have pulled

the door off its hinges, Herb balanced his strength with a cool head.

"It could be hard for you to race today from a jail cell," he observed.

"OK then, Herb, let's get the Toronto police down here! We'll all go over and just see what's in Raul's transporter."

Herb bit his lower lip and slowly shook his head.

"That won't work either. Even if the wings are in there, we couldn't prove they were ours, especially Rick's design. I made that one by hand from his drawings. Plus, there's no serial numbers or anything on them to identify them as ours. And even if Raul did take them, which wouldn't surprise me, by now both would be stripped of our decals and repainted. Rick's wing could already be bolted onto the back of his car."

I hated to admit it, but I knew that Herb was right. I sat down on one of the Swift's rear tires and rubbed my eyes. We were nowhere. We had suspicions, but nothing else. And even if Rick's wing was now part of DaSilva's car, he could simply say that his guys had made one just like ours because it was just such a great design. Happens all the time in racing. Nothing wrong with that.

Herb came back and sat down next to me on the other rear tire and checked his watch.

"OK, look. It's 7:15. Let's lock up the trailer, go back to the motor home, and make some coffee. The others will be here soon. Then we'll see what we can do."

I just stared out at the rain, wondering why this had to happen, and why there was nothing I could do about it. Yet.

Chapter 12

Men of the Race

The Formula Atlantic warm-up session was at 10:00 a.m. That allowed the teams to make any final adjustments before the race start at 1:00 p.m. Everyone had arrived at our pit by eight, and Herb briefed each of them on the break-in and theft of our wings. Reactions ranged from stunned disbelief to rage. Sophie was in shock, and Caroline and Susan Reynolds took her into the motor home to cook breakfast. It calmed her down. I was still game to go and have it out, face to face, with DaSilva, as were Rick and John Reynolds. But Herb and Allan were calm and firm. A confrontation might make us feel better, but it still wouldn't get us our wings back, even if DaSilva had them. We simply had no hard proof.

More importantly, we had no rear wing of any kind. And you don't just whip over to the nearest auto parts store and pick one up. Without a wing, we couldn't race at all. The car would not be drivable at racing speeds. What we did have was about two hours to try to do something about it.

The Swift had been brought out of the trailer and put up on stands next to the motor home. It was under an awning to keep it out of the rain. John Reynolds was pacing back and forth like a caged lion, with his fists clenched inside the pockets of his leather jacket and a face like thunder. Allan was on his cellphone; he was placing calls to everyone he knew, trying to find us a rear wing. As the Atlantic warm-up session began and then finished without us, we went through the usual preparations, more for something to do than because we were getting ready to race. Without a rear wing we knew we were going nowhere.

"Eedie!" a shrill voice came out of the gloom, then a small figure dashed under the awning and flipped back the hood of his yellow raincoat. Stefan Veilleux.

"Hey, Stefan," I said quietly. His usual elfish grin beamed from inside a frame of wild, curly black hair, but that soon faded as he looked around our pit and took in the grim expressions on everyone's faces.

"Eedie, you are missing the warm-up session. So, a thing is wrong. This I am feeling. Why does everyone's have the sad face?"

I gave Stefan the quick version of what had happened and even managed to leave out any mention of Raul. Stefan shook his head in disbelief.

"Swine! Pig dogs! Whoever does this thing, they are not men of the race. But—"

It's amazing what a single word can mean when you're looking for hope. Everybody stopped working and looked at the tiny Frenchman. He paced around the pit as he spoke.

"So. You are needs a rear wings, Eedie. And, I ask me, is there time for to make a new wings now? *Non.*"

Stefan liked to ask himself questions and then answer them, which seemed to help him with his English. Canada has two official languages—English and French. Stefan seemed to speak neither of them.

"And I, Stefan Veilleux, do I have a spare wings for my car? So you can asking me."

I played along. "OK. Stefan, do you have a spare wing?"

His face fell as he looked down at his wet shoes.

"*Non*, I have not a one." Then the elf smile returned as he stepped closer to me, held up five fingers and grinned broadly.

"I have four!" He glanced quickly at his hand and tucked in his thumb. "Yes! Four wing! And two of them, I am to giving for to you, Eedie. It is your pleasure!"

Rick and I jogged through the puddles with Stefan to his enormous blue transporter, where he quickly assembled his six-man crew. In rapid-fire French, he directed four of his guys to fetch two rear wings and told them to go back with Rick to our pit and fit one immediately to our Swift. Faced with such incredible generosity, I wasn't exactly sure what to do.

"Stefan, look. We just scored some major sponsorship, so I can pay you for these—"

"Pay?" Stefan cut me off, looking shocked.

"You thinks I want the pay, Eedie? *Non!* I am did this now for you. You are the friend to me. It is right to help, and it is wrong to steal. This I know from when I am the small boy. Also it is for the sport because, yes, I am a man of the race—not the swine dogs like these thieves! It is for honor that I lends you two wing. And, Eedie Stewart, would he do the same for his friend Stefan? *Oui*, yes, we know it. So, quick go now!"

Stefan Veilleux, the race pole-sitter and Formula Atlantic championship leader, had just lent his closest rival for this race—me—the parts I needed to start and maybe even beat him. In that moment I learned volumes about friendship, sportsmanship, and class. I'm not much for hugging other guys, but I almost crushed the tiny Frenchman right then and there.

Instead, I settled for a slap on the back and sprinted back to our pit.

We had half an hour to replace the wing and set up the Swift for a wet racetrack. Our pit became a flurry of activity. Four of Stefan's crewmen swarmed over the back of the car; Allan and Herb adjusted the suspension; Rick and Caroline set up the computers and timing equipment; and J.R. and I changed tires, checked fluids, and fueled the car. Somehow it all got done just as the track announcer called the Atlantic cars to assemble on the pre-grid. For a few minutes it even stopped raining. Things were definitely looking up.

Chapter 13

P1

I dashed into the motor home to suit up while everyone else pushed the car out from under the awning and onto the pre-grid. I got changed while inhaling a chicken salad sandwich that Sophie insisted I had to eat before I could go out and play. Then I grabbed my gloves, helmet, and shoe bag, and ran out the door. As I splashed through the puddles past the other teams' cars, I caught a glimpse of Raul DaSilva's crew strapping him in, but what really caught my eye was a big red tarp they had thrown over the back of their car. Very interesting. What did they have to hide?

"Eddie!" Herb yelled. "Let's go, man. Get in!"

I changed to my dry racing boots, and Herb almost threw me into the Swift. He helped me buckle up the six-point harness while Caroline passed me my helmet and gloves and Rick fired the engine. Allan passed me an umbrella to keep the rain off, and plugged the radio jack into my helmet.

"Edward, how do you read?"

I clicked the yellow Transmit button.

"Loud and clear. Hey did you see the tarp over the back of Raul's car? What do you want to bet—"

Allan held up his hand and shook his head. "Save that for later. All I want you to do for the next hour is settle down and concentrate on racing this fabulous car. Nothing else. And I shall stay off the radio for a while to let you do so. Understood?"

"Yes, Mr. Tanner, sir!" I replied with military precision, and saluted.

Allan raised an eyebrow. "No need to be cheeky, Edward."

He gave me a thumbs-up and backed away from the car as the official starter twirled his green flag signaling the field to get underway behind the BMW pace car. I snicked the gearbox into first and gently rolled the Swift forward with Stefan on my right and twenty-six other cars following behind. There is absolutely no better way to start a race than on the front row with a clear track ahead. The rain was reduced to a fine drizzle, but the track was glistening wet.

Small drops formed on my visor as we picked up

speed. I stayed well back of the BMW, and the airflow helped to keep my visor fairly clear, but I knew that would change the second I got behind someone. Better not to let that happen.

We did two pace laps to warm up the tires, and then they brought us to a stop on the pit-straight in grid positions for a standing start. Rolling starts were used on ovals like Milwaukee, but on a street or road course like Toronto, Atlantic cars started from a standstill.

When the green flag dropped, everyone buried the throttle and drag raced flat-out to the first corner. As the fastest qualifier, Stefan had his blue number 7 car in the pole position, which was on the inside of the front row to my right. As the second-fastest car, I was beside him on row one, and so on down the field to the slowest guys in row nineteen. Raul DaSilva and his teammate, Kurt Heinrich, were side by side right behind us on row two.

With the inside lane, Stefan would have the best shot at the first corner—a sharp right-hander. If he got there first, I'd be directly in the spray from his car and almost blind through turn one and out onto the long straight that was Lakeshore Boulevard. On the other hand, if I got a better start and beat him to turn one, I'd have the lead and a clear track ahead. In these conditions, whoever got into turn one and down the long straight first could very well control the entire race.

The starter raised the green flag, and twenty-eight throttles opened wide as we waited for the instant when he would drop the flag and unleash the pack. My eyes were glued to his right arm, watching for the first twitch of downward movement, when I suddenly saw Stefan's car lurch next to me. Its engine almost died, and in that same instant, the starter waved the green flag. I nailed the throttle, my Swift scrambled for traction for a few seconds, and then the tires bit. I lunged ahead of Stefan, accelerated hard to third gear, then snapped a downshift to second and turned into turn one, alone and in the lead.

As I powered down Lakeshore for the first time, I grabbed a quick glance in my mirrors. Through the plume of spray from my rear tires, I managed to pick out the bright blue nose of Stefan's car, about twenty feet back, in second. He had been a bit too anxious on the start and had almost stalled, but that mistake handed me a golden opportunity to build a lead with no traffic ahead and a clear field of vision. It was a huge break, and I took full advantage of it, running the Swift hard up through the gears and holding it wide open all the way down the long straight, through the tight, narrow walls of turn three, and then building speed again over the back part of the course. The car felt a bit lazy; but that was ideal for a slippery track surface, and I was able to control small slides easily.

As I flashed past the pits at the end of lap one, Herb held up the pit board.

P1
L2
+5

First place, lap two, and a five-second lead. Excellent. The rain had finally stopped, but the track and racing line remained wet, with some large puddles in a few places. The traction was actually quite good with the Yokohama rain tires, which used a soft, sticky rubber compound. Each tire also had five deep grooves, which had been hand-cut into the tread to channel the water away. Combined with front and rear wings set for maximum downforce, and with soft suspension settings, the Swift stuck well through the corners. I wondered how much better it would have been if I still had Rick's wing. The back end still wanted to dance out into oversteer when I put the power down, but on a street track like Toronto, that was actually a faster way out of the many tight corners. And nothing is more fun in a race car than long power slides.

The radio was quiet for the first five laps, as Allan allowed me to focus all of my concentration on building a lead. By the time I came past the pits to start lap seven, Herb's board told me that I had a full fifteen seconds on Stefan in second place. The rain continued to hold off, and with no one visible in my mirrors, and no one ahead, I felt like I was the only car on the track. Just keep it up for another twenty laps or so, I told myself, and we're home free. Piece of cake.

Allan came over the radio. "Edward, do you read?"

"Go, Allan."

"Place one. Lap seven. Plus fifteen."

"I love it!"

"No doubt, Edward. But listen now. Settle down. Track's drying out fast. Start saving the tires."

"OK."

I knew what he meant, and it snapped me back to reality. This race wasn't even close to being over, and tires, not just driving, might very well decide it.

The slick tires that we usually run are engineered for maximum grip on hot, dry pavement, but on a wet surface slicks float up on top of the water and hydroplane. This means wheel-spin, locked brakes, and almost no cornering grip. It's like driving on ice with bald tires. So on a wet track, teams use rain tires or wets, which are excellent in...well, the rain. But they are truly awful on a warm, dry track, like this one was fast becoming. The rubber compound is too soft to last very long, and the deeply-grooved tread tends to make the car squirm as the tires overheat. That can happen quickly. It gets to the point where the tire starts to *chunk* and throw off entire pieces of rubber as the tread disintegrates. When the tires reach that stage, you really lose grip; the wheels go way out of balance; the car becomes almost undrivable at racing speeds; and your speed drops drastically. If my set of wets started to overheat, that comfortable lead could easily disappear in minutes.

As every team had started the race with rain tires, I figured that we all had, basically, three options. First option was to stay out on wets and hope it started to rain again; but from the way the sky was clearing, more rain looked very unlikely. Option two was to stay out on wets on a drying track, try to save the tires, and survive the remaining twenty laps without dropping back. That was a long time, and it would require a much different driving style. The tire temperatures could be kept down if I drove through puddles off the racing line and eased up on my cornering speeds. Both tactics might be enough to keep the rain tires together until the finish, but it would cost me time every lap and could seriously erode my lead.

Option three was to dive into the pits for a set of four slick tires, which would be ideal as the track dried, but that decision presented some major problems. Any time spent stopped in the pits to change four wheels would definitely cost me the lead and probably even drop me out of the top five. And I realized that we had never made a pit stop with this car. Not even a practice.

That's when I started to worry.

Chapter 14

Men of the Race

We had all the equipment needed to jack up the car and quickly change over to a fresh set of slicks, but a lightning-quick pit stop would be new territory for us. Compared to race distances for Champ Cars or NASCAR stock cars, Formula Atlantic races were relatively short. Under normal circumstances, the cars didn't stop for fuel or fresh tires; and if you did, there was usually no time left to get back near the front. Pit stops were rare in this series, but I wished that we had at least practiced one before today. It was time to talk to the boss, and I keyed the radio as I entered the long back-straight to complete lap nine.

"Hey, Allan!"

"Go, Edward."

"Should I come in for slicks?"

"No! Stay out. Let's see what develops. If we get a yellow, I might bring you in. Save the tires for now."

"OK."

There were twenty-seven other cars behind me, and twenty-seven other race engineers asking themselves the same questions: Stay out on wets or come in for slicks? Or wait and see if the rain returned? Allan wanted to be patient. If there was an accident back in the pack, the whole field would be put under a yellow caution flag. That meant that everyone had to slow down and lap slowly in single file behind the pace car. No passing allowed. If I pitted under yellow, I would lose the lead, but if it was a long enough caution period, I could come into the pits under yellow, change to slicks and re-enter the track behind the pace car, still near the front.

I did six more laps, checking all the time for anyone coming up in my mirrors. But I remained all alone in the lead. I felt great about that, but I was really beginning to worry about the vibrations starting to come back through the steering wheel. The Swift didn't want to brake straight or turn-in cleanly anymore. I'd been trying to preserve the rain tires by driving through puddles and easing up a bit in the corners, but I knew that they were going away fast. When I came past the pits to start lap seventeen, Caroline was holding up the board instead of Herb, and it confirmed what I had feared.

P1

L17

+7

My lead was down to seven seconds. I was losing the lead every time around, and I'd soon be caught and passed, some time in the next seven or eight laps. Maybe sooner. The sun was actually starting to come out, so the rain was gone for good. While the road surface was still damp, the racing line was almost dry. The car's handling was getting worse by the minute, and as the rain tires started to disintegrate, the vibrations became so bad that it was difficult to focus my eyes at high speed. I was afraid that I wasn't even going to finish, let alone win this thing, if I didn't get a set of slicks soon. We were running out of time waiting for a yellow. I wondered if some of the others had already come in for slicks, or if they were just going for broke, which could explain why they were eating into my lead. I started down the long Lakeshore straight for the seventeenth time and keyed the radio.

"Allan!"

"Go, Edward."

"It's really getting bad. I'm losing time everywhere!"

"I know. I'm watching you on the ESPN feed. Stay out. Try and nurse it."

"OK!"

Nurse it? The only way I could hold the Swift steady down any of the high-speed straights was with a death grip on the steering wheel, which now felt like a jack hammer. I braked and grabbed first gear for turn three at the end of the straight, turned in as gently as possible, and promptly spun clean around to the left and came to a stop facing the wrong way in the middle of the corner. Just like that. Allan was on the radio instantly.

"Edward! Do you have power?"

"Yes! Still running!"

Somehow I had performed the correct foot reaction to a spin, pushing in the clutch with my left foot while braking and rolling onto the throttle with my right to keep the engine running. If the engine had stalled, I'd have been done, as the small onboard battery wouldn't restart it.

"Good lad! Get moving! Slowly back to the pits now, I think you may have a puncture. Left rear."

I cranked the wheel hard-left and gave it a burst of throttle, snapping the Swift around to face the right way. Slowly I began to pick up some speed. I glanced in my mirror and confirmed from its profile that the left rear tire was going flat and turning to toast. In fact, it was burnt toast and starting to fly apart, throwing chunks of rubber high into the air. I was going to get my set of slicks, but first I had to limp back to the pits, staying in first gear all the way from turn three to the pit entrance at turn ten half a lap ahead. Any faster, and I'd lose the tire completely and be running on the wheel rim, which would certainly damage the rear suspension and finish me for good. I crawled along, watching my mirrors, waiting for the pack to pounce.

It didn't take them long.

Three corners later they were on me, howling past as if I was standing still, led by Stefan Veilleux, then Raul DaSilva, Kurt Heinrich, and three others. I smashed my fist on the steering wheel as I watched myself go from first to seventh in a matter of seconds. I crept through turns eight and nine and finally saw the pit entrance. Allan was ready.

"Nice and easy now, Edward. Look for Herb. Hit the marks."

I motored along the pit lane almost on the wheel rim and turned into our race pit. With the engine running, I stopped the Swift right on the white guide marks. J.R. rammed a lever jack under the rear wing and popped the back of the car off the ground while

Allan did the same at the front. Herb and Rick attacked the rear of the Swift with air wrenches, zipping off the single center nut that held each wheel and replacing it with a fresh wheel and race slick. They tightened the new rear wheels, Caroline rolled two new slicks to them, and they leapt to the front and repeated the procedure. The jacks were released and yanked away, the car dropped to the ground, and Allan yelled into his headset.

"Go! Go! Go! Stay in first! Watch your speed!"

The engine screamed as I popped the clutch and blasted out of the pit with both rear tires smoking furiously. The pit lane had a speed limit of sixty miles per hour, which I got to in about three seconds flat. I held it in first until I was back onto the racetrack and then took it hard up to second gear, then through the tight right-hander and onto Lakeshore Boulevard again. It seemed like a good stop, but I had to know.

"Allan!"

"Yes, Edward! Go." He sounded out of breath.

"How long?"

"Sophie timed it. Twenty-five seconds for tires. About fifty total, counting coming in and getting out again."

Not too bad for our first-ever pit stop.

"Good job, you guys! OK, where are we?"

There was a long pause before Allan came back.

"Lap eighteen. Nine to go. By my chart, you're eleventh."

Ouch.

Chapter 15

This Is Going to Get Interesting

A few minutes ago I had been leading the race with a comfortable cushion, and I was starting to see myself stepping up on the podium for my first Formula Atlantic victory. Piece of cake, I thought then. That fantasy was out the window now, as I was down in eleventh place. I was at least thirty seconds behind the lead group, with only nine laps left. I'd just had a wake-up call as to how fast things can change in racing. Getting on the podium today looked like a real long shot.

The Swift's Cosworth engine made 300 horsepower, and I wanted all of it. I had to move back up to the front. New racing slicks, however, need at least a full lap to get some heat into them and produce maximum grip, and then they stick like glue. I had to be patient and take it easy on lap eighteen. Once the tires were warm I'd be ready to fly. But trying to go flat-out too soon, on cold slicks, would guarantee another spin and very likely end my day up against one of the barriers that lined the Toronto course. I'd already had my fill of concrete walls.

Waiting for the tires to come in gave me a minute or so to take stock of the situation. It wasn't over yet. Thanks to Herb's suspension work, I knew that I could out-brake anyone, the engine was strong, and I still had a pretty good handling race car even without Rick's wing. And I was likely one of the few drivers who had exactly the right tires for a dry racetrack. There was no way to know for sure how many of the guys ahead of me might have also changed to slicks, if they were still racing hard on disintegrating wets, or if they were cruising around just trying to make it to the finish on bad tires. It was a good bet that most of them had elected to stay out on rain tires, nursing their ill-handling cars and trying to finish without the penalty of a pit stop. Once my slicks started to bite, I'd have nine laps to find out if I was right.

As I flashed past the pits to start lap nineteen, Herb's board gave me the information I needed:

P11
L19
− 2

Eleventh place, lap nineteen of twenty-seven, two seconds behind the tenth-place car, which I was already catching rapidly. The tires were almost up to prime operating temperature, and I was getting good traction again. I blew by him easily, halfway down the straight, and then caught two cars running nose-to-tail in eighth and ninth. I noted that both of them still had their grooved rain tires on. I tucked in tight behind them as we entered the braking area, then darted to the inside, leaving my braking to the last second, managing to squeeze past both of them going into turn three.

Running hard onto the back part of the course, I caught sight of the next group of three cars, also running nose-to-tail in fifth, sixth, and seventh places. Again, on my fresh slicks, I reeled them in quickly. By the time we passed the pits to complete the lap, I was close enough to see the grooves in their tires. They too were still running on well-worn rain tires. Maybe I was the only car out on slicks; if that was true, I had a major advantage.

Wide-open down Lakeshore at 160 mph on lap twenty, I had already mapped out how to out-brake the seventh-place car, maybe even the car in sixth as well. It might have worked, too, until the guy leading the group ahead of me locked his brakes at the end of the straight and lost it big time.

His bright red car pitched sideways, smacked the left barrier hard, and then shot back across the track, straight into the path of the other two. One of them hit his front wheel and became airborne, while the other guy, in a black car, swerved violently but hit the red car broadside, shearing off its rear wing. I had a front-row seat for all of this from about twenty feet behind, and everything just seemed to roll into slow motion. I watched as the car that had been launched sailed slowly through the air while the black car spun lazily to the right. The poor guy who had lost control and started all the carnage ground to a halt next to the barrier, in a cloud of smoke and steam. It was like watching a disaster movie frame by frame. Except that I was in it.

There was no time to think about what to do, only to react. I braked hard, eased the Swift right, flicked left to avoid a piece of wing, then right again to miss the spinning black car. I found myself through the accident, out of the corner, and accelerating hard up to turn four. Allan was on the radio instantly.

"Edward! Everything OK?"

"OK! Got through in one piece!"

"Feel it out carefully. You may have cut a tire. Course is going full yellow."

"OK."

All of the corner marshals were furiously waving double yellow caution flags at the drivers. I automatically lifted my foot off the accelerator and cruised the back side of the course. Then I came around again and passed the scene of the accident that I had narrowly escaped the lap before. A dozen marshals had immediately dragged the three wrecked cars out of harm's way and were already sweeping up the debris. I caught a quick glimpse of the drivers standing together. I was thankful that none of them had been injured, and that some very talented engineers had built such deceptive strength into Formula Atlantic cars.

Having driven through a whirlwind of broken metal and fiberglass, I could easily have picked up something sharp in one of the tires. I circled gently to ensure that I didn't have another puncture, then keyed the radio as I passed the pits to start lap twenty-two.

"Everything feels OK, Allan."

"Good. Relax for a bit. This is going to get interesting."

"Where am I?"

"Fifth. Close up on the leaders."

Chapter 16

Justice

A full-course yellow was exactly what I needed. This race was about to change dramatically. Again. With its roof lights flashing to signal everyone to reduce speed and form up single file, the BMW pace car went out in front of the leader, Stefan Veilleux. No passing. In other words, no racing until the track was cleared. I hoped this would take only a lap or two, but it could possibly take all of the remaining five. It also meant that whatever cushion Stefan had built up would disappear as the rest of the field caught up to him behind the pace car. Best of all, from where I was sitting, if the track could be cleared and racing allowed to resume, I was sure I had the best car in the field to take one last shot at that victory podium.

By the end of lap twenty-three, I was relieved to

have caught up to the front runners. Stefan was leading, followed by Raul DaSilva, a new Italian driver named Elio Bennedetto in third, and Raul's teammate, Kurt Heinrich, in fourth. Relief quickly grew into confidence as I drew close enough to confirm that all of them had gambled and stayed out on wet tires, while I was now on dry slicks. Our pit stop had given me the edge.

The marshals had everything cleaned up in turn three at the end of the straight. The pace car was still out, but its roof lights had been switched off, which indicated that it would be returning to the pits and that we would get a green flag to resume racing. Allan saw it, too.

"Going green, Edward. Going green. Three laps left. Stay sharp."

"OK."

The BMW pulled into the pits, and the starter immediately gave us a waved green flag. The field crossed the start/finish line to begin the final three laps. I was hard on the throttle instantly and pulled up tightly behind Kurt Heinrich's Ascension Motorsports car in fourth. He was Raul's teammate, a very fast guy, and I knew that getting past him was going to be tough.

As a spectator, I'd seen Kurt Heinrich's driving a

month earlier at Laguna Seca, California. As a competitor, I'd seen him at Milwaukee. And now, here in Toronto, I knew what his role was. Stay behind his boss, Raul DaSilva, and do whatever was necessary, including outright blocking, to make sure that Raul was protected from anyone trying to catch him. In a way, it was too bad. I thought that Heinrich could be a fine race driver, maybe even a title contender, if he'd been with a different team. But there would be no championship dreams for any driver who was Raul's teammate.

I closed right up on Heinrich and took a close look at his rear wing. I was still sure that Ascension Motorsports was behind the theft of our wings, so it was a bit of a disappointment to find that Kurt's wing was the standard Swift design, not Rick's unique profile. His car was sliding around on badly worn rain tires, and I began to work out where I might be able to try an out-braking maneuver. I figured that he wouldn't make it easy for me. I knew that I'd have to wait until we finished this lap and got onto a long straight again before I could make a move.

But there was no waiting.

To my complete surprise, Heinrich pulled to the left, stuck his right hand out of the cockpit and pointed to the open lane beside his car. He was indicating that he knew I was behind him and that he was moving over and allowing me to pass. Was this the gesture of a sportsman, or was it something else? It could easily have been a trap to set up a collision and remove me as a threat to Raul.

There wasn't time to wait another half-lap to figure it out. I wanted to have any chance at catching the leaders, so I held my breath, accepted Heinrich's invitation, and pulled the Swift alongside as we both braked for turn eight. He stayed wide on my left and provided me with ample room to pass, and as I did so, I waved briefly to thank him, glanced in my mirror and saw his orange glove wave back. It had almost been too easy. But I wasn't complaining, as I was now back up to fourth place and had Bennedetto directly in my sights. I easily caught and passed his ill-handling car on the pit-straight. I looked ahead hungrily for Raul's yellow car.

I started the second-last lap in third place. Allan was with me.

"Lap twenty-six, Edward. One more after this. Gap is seven. Gap is seven."

"OK!"

Raul and Stefan Veilleux were racing hard together, about fifty feet ahead. But their cars were darting nervously all over the track on their worn tires.

Clearly they had gambled and stayed out on wets. I easily halved the distance as we swept down the long Lakeshore straight. I was finally close enough to Raul to get a good look at his rear wing. This time there was no disappointment and no doubt. The proof was staring me in the face. Raul was definitely running our wing. He had stolen Rick's design and Herb's workmanship. It had been repainted bright yellow, but I knew instantly that it was ours. No wonder they had it covered up before the race started.

This had become a fight to the finish. The Toronto race fans knew it too; the sold-out crowd was on its feet as I finished that lap. I was going to try everything I knew to pass Raul. It was my job—plus, I really hated to lose. So I really didn't need any extra motivation to put DaSilva down a place. But looking at that wing took my determination to a new level. Passing him had now become more than hard-nosed racing. It even went beyond payback for his constant put-downs and slimy arrogance. This was something new, something higher and better. I felt that I had been put at that exact time and place to set things right, to exact justice. And to teach Raul and his team of thugs the ageless lesson that, in the end, bullies, thieves, cheats, and liars always finish up the same way. Losers.

I had daydreamed about how sweet it would be to pass DaSilva, but I knew that he'd make it as tough as possible for me. I charged, hard, down the inside of the braking zone for turn three. As expected, Raul swerved over violently to block the line, giving me no room at all. So I decided to create a little racing room the way I used to in my Trans-Am Mustang. I eased up just a touch on my braking and allowed the nose of my car to nudge his right rear wheel. Just a little tap to say hello. It wasn't hard enough to push him off or damage either of our cars, but it startled Raul enough to make him run just a little wider on the exit of the corner than he should have. That gave me enough space to get alongside, then gradually pull ahead through turns four and five.

I was in front of Raul, but he stormed right back. He flew past the front of my car in a wild passing attempt as we braked for turn eight. He wouldn't even have made it on fresh slicks, never mind badly worn rain tires, and I seriously wondered if he was out to ram into me rather than take back second place.

Whatever Raul was thinking, he was wildly out of control. All four of his wheels were locked up, and his tires were smoking. He slid past on my inside, trying to stop before he hit the tire barrier.

He lost.

He slid past my nose and speared into the barrier, nose first, covering his car in a pile of old tires.

I powered out of the turn. Sweet indeed. I keyed the radio. "Allan! Tell Rick and Herb that was for them!"

"They know! Gap is six. Lead car is smoking. Last lap. Last lap! It's your race, Edward!"

"OK."

Stefan and I began the final lap. As I closed up on him, I confirmed what Allan's sharp eye had seen from the pits. His car was blowing plumes of thick, blue oil smoke out of its exhaust pipe. As I got closer, I could smell it. Tiny droplets of oil spattered my visor. These were terminal signs; his engine was about to quit.

Stefan must have pushed everything well past the limit to stay in the lead, but he was paying for it now. He would be lucky to finish the lap before losing the engine. I, on the other hand, had the strongest car in the race—and an excellent chance of either passing him to take the win, or picking up the lead if his car died.

I was pumped and hungry for the win, but at the same time I found myself almost cheering the tiny Frenchman on, rather than wanting to take the lead away from him. As much as I had wanted Raul to lose, I wouldn't have minded all that much if Stefan won. I wouldn't have been in the race at all if he hadn't lent me his wing. Raul deserved what he got; he'd earned it. And in the same way I felt that Stefan should also get what he had earned. His kindness should have been repaid with a win. That only seemed fair, but sometimes things don't always balance out quite that nicely.

Stefan's smoking engine finally died going into turn six on the last lap, and he coasted to a stop as I accelerated past and into the lead. Four corners later I came onto the start/finish straight for the last time. The starter gave me the checkered flag, and I saw our entire crew leaning over the pit guardrail going nuts.

I crossed the line with both arms in the air and almost lost control of the car. It wouldn't have been terribly professional of me to have crashed on the victory lap.

Chapter 17

Winner's Circle

For a driver, the cool-down lap after the checkered flag is a time when emotions that have been held in check during a race are finally released. If you have made some bonehead decisions or driven poorly, there is time for you to yell at yourself and curse in the privacy of your race car. On the other hand, if you've done well, you have a few minutes to relax and bathe in the satisfaction that comes from hard work and intense concentration. And if you've done really well, perhaps won, then it becomes one of those golden moments when all the frustrations, expense, boredom, long nights, and days of numbing travel are forgotten. Instantly, it's all worth it.

Toronto was golden for me. I flipped up my helmet visor, drank deeply from the rush of cool, humid air, and cruised around the track. I waved to acknowledge the applause of the corner marshals and the fans. My first victory as a professional. As I rounded turn six again, I saw Stefan slowly shuffling away from his dead car, head down, helmet in hand, as he began the long, sad walk back to the pits. He looked destroyed. I just had to do something other than cruise by and wave in victory. I pulled the Swift over next to him and stopped. He turned, grinned broadly, and leaned over the cockpit, shouting above the engine's open exhaust.

"Eedie! You win! You are the man!"

"Thanks to you, buddy! Hey, want a lift back?"

"*Oui*, yes!"

It was a bizarre idea, but I thought that a really cool way to finish the victory lap would be for us to return to the pits together, with me driving and Stefan perched on the side of my car. He curled up on the left-side pod, grabbed hold of the roll bar, and gave me a pat on the helmet to signal he was ready. I drove slowly back to the pits while Stefan pointed to pretty girls in the crowd and blew kisses at them.

I parked the Swift in the winner's circle and shut down the engine. Stefan hopped off. He helped me unplug the radio and release the safety harness. I climbed out of the Swift, and this time I bear-hugged the guy. Just crushed him—in a manly way, of course.

Then I held him by the shoulders and looked him straight in the eye.

"Stefan. I would not be here right now if it wasn't for you."

Stefan shrugged off the compliment and grinned broadly.

"I am not for knowing this? If I am not to win, then it is for you that we are as happy as I am for me and for you also. But go now, Eedie. Enjoy!"

I helped the officials push the Swift into the impound area. The top three cars were automatically impounded and checked by the series technical inspectors, to make sure that everything about them was legal. Technical disqualifications were rare but not unheard of. Any team had thirty minutes if they wanted to file a protest against a winning car. The results wouldn't be official for half an hour, but that didn't stop the podium celebrations from getting underway.

Quite a crowd had assembled in front of the victory stage. It felt incredible to step up onto the center pedestal of the podium for the first time as the race winner. Kurt Heinrich was on my left, as the third-place finisher, and a beaming Elio Bennedetto—who had finished second in this, his first Atlantic race—was on my right. We waved, posed for pictures with our trophies, and kidded around. Elio had Italian movie-star good looks and a brilliant smile, which he was using to great effect with the press photographers and throngs of female fans.

Kurt seemed to be in a lighter mood than after his win at Milwaukee, but he looked terrible, with a split lip, an ugly cut across his nose, and a blackened eye. Each of us got large magnums of champagne. I don't drink, so there was only one thing to do. I'd learned my victory-podium lesson well, at Milwaukee. Champagne was not for drinking. With a nod and a wink to Kurt, we shook our bottles violently, popped the corks, surrounded the unsuspecting Bennedetto, and blasted him square in the face from both sides. We showed no mercy; he never had a chance.

The champagne caught him just as he was frozen in another hero-driver fashion pose for a photographer. It blew off his sponsor's baseball cap and instantly drenched him in a sparkling white crossfire. Champagne really stings when it gets in your eyes, and our surprise assault temporarily blinded him. Elio fired back wildly with his bottle, but as he couldn't see anything, his return fire had no effect. He decided to retreat, staggered several steps backward, and promptly stepped straight off the edge of the podium.

Fortunately, his fall was broken by a perfectly placed green plastic garbage barrel, which he hit squarely and went straight into, butt end first. Kurt and I went to the edge of the stage, peered over, and saw him wedged firmly inside the barrel with only his feet, head, and arms sticking out above the rim. We just couldn't leave him blind and trapped in a garbage can. We jumped down, rolled the barrel onto its side, and pulled him out. Elio's gleaming white driving suit was covered with large wet blotches of mustard, ketchup, relish, various soda, and milkshake stains; and he had a half-eaten cheeseburger stuck to his chest. He was stunned, dripping wet, blind, and speechless. But he still had that grin.

"Welcome to Canada, Elio," I said, steering him over to where his crew was waiting.

Kurt and I collected our trophies, picked up our helmets, and started to walk over to the Race Control office to collect our prize money. I knew that first place paid $20,000, and I also knew that a chunk of that was going to get spent tonight on my team in the best restaurant in Toronto. I was already thinking about where we could go that wouldn't involve pancakes, when Kurt took my arm and stopped me.

"Stewart, may we talk please?" he asked quietly. "It is important."

"Sure. And make it Eddie," I replied.

"OK, Eddie. My car is just over there."

We walked a short distance to the competitors' parking area. Kurt took a tiny remote out of his driving suit pocket, pointed it at a new black Porsche 911 Carrera, and disarmed the security system. As I walked around to the passenger side, I noted that it had orange Florida plates. I couldn't put my finger on it right then, but this car looked familiar. I knew I'd seen it before. We climbed in, powered down the windows, and Kurt took a package of German cigarettes out of the glove box. His hands shook as he lit one, inhaled deeply, then offered the package to me. I declined.

"I have wanted to talk to you since before the Milwaukee race, but I was not free to do so," he said in flawless English.

"I'm listening now," I replied.

"Today was my last race in Formula Atlantic. I leave tonight for Germany to look for a new team. We may not meet again. And so, before I go, I must set some things straight with you. I will tell you them once, here in private, and never again."

Chapter 18

Respect

I was sitting next to the driver who, after finishing second today, had to be considered the favorite to win the North American Formula Atlantic championship. I'd already done the math in my head. Kurt Heinrich was in the best position for the title, with only the final race in Miami left to run. And he was walking away from that? And what did he need to settle with me? It didn't add up.

"I don't get it, Kurt. What's going on?"

He smiled weakly and took another long drag on his cigarette.

"A return to Germany is not my first choice, Eddie. I would like very much to do the last race in Miami and perhaps win this championship. But I cannot. Raul has...he has made other plans. With him, it was never my job to win races. My victory in Milwaukee last month was not supposed to happen. And today he screamed and yelled at me all morning, to make sure I remembered that my job, my only job, was to help him to win."

I looked again at his shaking hands and the cuts and bruises on his face, and I knew that a lot more than just shouting had gone on inside Raul's Ascension Motorsports transporter.

"I was instructed to make sure that you or Stefan did not win today. Once I had done that, and Raul was in the lead, I was to stop my car before the end of the race. Pretend that it was damaged."

I nodded. "So the plan was for none of the championship contenders to score points, except Raul."

"Precisely. But as things turned out, this did not happen. The rain stopped. You spun. Stefan drove brilliantly. There was the full-course yellow; Bennedetto came from nowhere, and then you returned to challenge for the lead on slicks. Incredible!"

Kurt shook his head and managed a weak laugh.

"You forgot something else, Kurt. You let me through into fourth place. You could have easily held me up, and Raul might have caught Stefan and won the race instead of me. But you didn't."

Kurt ground out his cigarette in the ashtray.

"I could not do it. If you were challenging, my orders were to hold you up and, if necessary, take us both out. Set up a collision and make it look like a racing accident."

"I wondered about that when you moved over. You could have put us both into the wall with a flick of your wrist. Why didn't you?"

Kurt looked at me for a long moment and then turned away, staring blankly through the windshield.

"I came to Ascension Motorsports three months ago as a professional racing driver, Eddie. When I signed my contract with Raul's team, he promised me a fair opportunity to succeed. Equal cars. No team orders. Let the best man win. But it was not long before I saw that it was all lies. And when I looked at myself in the mirror before I got into my car today, I saw what I had become. A bodyguard, a cheat, a liar. Also, a coward. I was ashamed. And then, this morning, he told me that if I failed to execute his plan, I was finished. Fired. I almost quit before the start, but I decided to do the race anyway. I thought I might be able to put some things right."

"Like what?"

He took a second cigarette from the package, lit it, and inhaled sharply.

"Like the theft of your rear wings last night. I suspect you know now that it was Ascension crew members, acting on Raul's orders, who stole them from your trailer. You must have recognized the wing that was fitted to Raul's car today. I did not want to see him profit from that."

"You're right. I suspected all along that it was Raul or his guys. Today confirmed it. The only reason we made the race at all was because Stefan lent us a spare wing."

Kurt nodded and glanced at his watch. His hands had stopped shaking and his voice seemed calmer.

"Yes, Stefan would do that. He is a gentleman, or—what is it he likes to say—a man of the race. I must leave soon, Eddie. But before I go, understand a few other things. Raul puts on an aggressive face, but inside he is weak, as all bullies are. He is afraid that he is not good enough, and he is especially afraid of drivers who are. Like Stefan, me, and especially you. So he uses force; he cheats, steals, and lies. More correctly, he gets others to do it for him. And he trusts no one. I and a crewman were even assigned to watch Allan Tanner, after he left Raul for your team, to see what he was up to. We were even told to follow you from California. We actually took photographs of your wing models on the roof of your motor home."

Then it clicked. A new black Porsche Carrera, with Florida plates, had tailed us outside of Chicago on our way across country to our first race in Milwaukee.

That had been Kurt and a crewman, snapping pictures of Rick's wing models as he was trying to test them on the motor home's roof at highway speeds. I had to laugh at that; it was so bizarre.

Kurt also found a moment to chuckle. "You know, Raul actually had his crew try to build those wings from the photographs we took, but they could not do it. But when he saw how well the design worked for you in the Milwaukee race, he became desperate. He decided it would be much better for him if you lost the advantage of your wing—and he got it all for himself. If he could not build his own, he would simply steal yours. This is how Raul thinks, how he does things. The man has no conscience."

I sat in silence for a minute and processed what Kurt had revealed. It all fit. In Raul's mind, there were no rules, no such thing as right and wrong, and no guilt. There was only what he wanted, and what he had to do to get it.

Kurt stubbed out his second cigarette, opened the door, and stepped out of the Porsche. I got out, closed my door, and leaned on the roof.

"Thanks, Kurt. I appreciate this."

He nodded. "It was difficult to tell you these things. Difficult, but necessary. You deserve to know the truth, Eddie. What you choose to do with it is now up to you. As for me, I have no excuse for my behavior. I offer you my apology. I hope that there will be no hard feelings between us."

"None. Apology accepted. Just one question, though. Why did you go along with it?"

Kurt sighed heavily.

"Money. Always for me it is the money. I do not come from a wealthy family like Raul or Stefan. I came to America to make enough money to go back to Germany and start my own team. Raul offered me $50,000 per race, with a $250,000 bonus if I helped him win the championship. I thought that I could silence my conscience and do that. I found that I was wrong."

I extended my hand and we shook firmly. Then he re-armed the Porsche's security system. We left the parking compound, picked up our checks from Race Control, and stopped for a moment outside the pit building.

"Well, you might not get that team together right away, Kurt, but I think you'll sleep better tonight."

"Yes, perhaps. I sleep a little better because you now understand who you are up against. Raul failed today, but he will have a new second driver for Miami, and the crew is making modifications to his car. I overheard them whispering something about the fuel injection, but I did not hear the details. He will hold nothing back. Good luck, Eddie Stewart. You are a fine driver. Perhaps we will compete again under better circumstances."

I watched the tall German walk away and disappear into the pit-lane crowds. Kurt Heinrich had made some mistakes, and he knew it. But he was no whiner, and he wasn't trying to blame someone else or deflect the responsibility. He faced up to his mistakes squarely and was trying to put things right again. I had to respect that.

The city of Toronto has a large Italian section filled with great restaurants, and that night I took the whole team to three of them—one for appetizers, one for the main course, and the third one for dessert. Sophie was thrilled. She tasted samples from everyone's plates and spent most of the evening in the restaurant kitchens, talking furiously in Italian with the chefs, swapping restaurant stories and trading recipes. Sophie and Susan Reynolds were even invited into the kitchen to help prepare the main course. Despite a complete lack of anything resembling a pancake in Italian cuisine, Herb still managed to put away double servings of everything.

One of the restaurants had a karaoke machine, which Rick used to perform a riveting version of his favorite Elvis song, "Burning Love," fearlessly backed up by Allan and Herb. They received thunderous applause and did two encores. I flatly refused to join them in "Viva Las Vegas." Instead, I took the stage and tried to give a short thank you speech to the team, until I was pelted by a hail of dinner rolls, which sent me back to my seat. Caroline found all of this delightful, and she snapped away constantly with her digital camera. She got a full record of the weekend to email to our parents and for our team's expanding website. It was a great evening, fueled by excellent food, constant laughter, and the energy that came from the rapid success of our small team. We were filled with the kind of confidence that only winning can provide.

Somewhere past midnight, enjoying the warm, summer night, we drifted back to our hotel. Caroline and I brought up the rear of our group, which was fine with me. Everyone had spent the night discussing the race and Raul, renamed the Thief of Toronto. But I'd had enough. There was a time when I had been ready to punch his lights out, but now I was glad that I'd kept my head. For all of his slimeball treachery, Raul had still finished up stuffed into the tire wall. It was exactly what he deserved. It was time to let it go.

I was becoming much more interested in focusing my energies in a new direction, which had been pressing in upon my mind for the past month—such as the exact shade of blue in Caroline's eyes, and how her long blonde hair fell gracefully over her shoulders as she strolled quietly beside me. And why our hands seemed to have slipped together.

Chapter 19

Herb's Reminder

Traveling from Toronto, Ontario, to the final race in Miami, Florida, would be another major cross-continent haul. This time we would cover over 1,700 miles heading south. Herb, Caroline, and I took the big Dodge crew cab and trailer. Following us in the motor home were Rick, Allan, and Sophie. Caroline spent a lot of time on the cellphone, talking to J.R. in New York and hashing out the details for some sort of special project that DynaSport was working up for the race team. I had no idea what it was; Caroline refused give me any details beyond how generous she thought the idea was.

We had two weeks until the final race, which would be on the 1.5-mile oval at Homestead Motorsport Park, a multi-million-dollar complex near Miami. J.R. and Susan Reynolds owned a vacation home in

Miami Beach. The plan was for us to meet up with them there, by the weekend. We'd relax and power tan for a few days, and then drive down to Homestead to set up shop by the middle of race week.

We got packed up and were underway early Monday. We crossed the Canada/US. border at Buffalo, New York, and then went on to Pittsburgh by nightfall. As a lasting and touching tribute, Herb had made me a small triangular trophy out of a piece of the aluminum wing that I'd smashed at Milwaukee, and he had glued it to the dashboard of the truck. Riveted to the top was a little candy-apple red plastic formula car, which I was certain had come out of one of Herb's cereal boxes. He only bought cereal that had prizes inside. Underneath, he had crudely printed the Formula Atlantic points leaders in black felt marker:

> 1. *Heinrich*
> 2. *DaSilva*
> 3. *Fast Eddie*
> 4. *Stefan*

Herb was truly gifted at building race cars, but this thing looked like it had been done by a group of four-year-olds wearing blindfolds. That didn't matter to the Man of Steel; it was the message that was important.

"This is a reminder, Eddie. For the next five days, you just look at this and remember that you're a pro race driver now. Maybe even a champion in a couple of weeks. It could happen, just like I said. And every minute you're in the truck, this baby will remind you of that."

Herb took a tissue and carefully wiped a speck of dust off the tiny plastic car.

"Thanks, Herb. It's really, uh…what's this wire coming out of the back?"

"I put a little light bulb inside the toy car and connected it to the truck's signal lights. Every time you turn or change lanes, it flashes right along with the turn signals. Go ahead, try it!"

Unfortunately, it worked perfectly, filling the cab with an eerie green glow every half-second.

"Well, it's…it's really bright, isn't it?" I observed.

"Yeah, I know! Should be fantastic at night. Anyway, I knew you'd like it, Eddie. Now, I think I'll go back for a quick snooze."

"Right. See you in Miami."

I knew that Herb would be in hibernation in the back of the crew cab for the next four days, which gave me lots of time to find something to cover it up with, or to find a pair of wire cutters.

After spending the night in the motor home near

Pittsburgh, we headed out before sunrise, rolled through Baltimore and got into Washington, D.C., by noon. As we were, after all, in the nation's capital, all of us felt that we should do the tourist thing, especially Allan and Sophie. So we parked our vehicles at an RV campground, called a cab, and spent the afternoon and evening taking in the sights. Sophie insisted that I take a picture of her in front of the White House, which I did—even though her enormous, plastic-fruit hat blocked out most of it.

Herb slept right through to our third day, which was blisteringly hot. We continued due south through Richmond, Virginia, and then into Florence, South Carolina, where the heat finally did in the radiator on the motor home. We found an old, faded radiator shop run by the three Carter Brothers (it said so on the faded sign). The Carters were well over seventy, but they quickly whipped out the failed radiator, chucked it on a heap of rusted parts, and then built us a better one, right there, from scratch.

I watched Sophie and Caroline comfortably dozing under a tree out front with a redbone coon hound at their feet. I wondered how they managed in the intense heat and humidity. I was soaked to the skin. One of the Carter brothers read my thoughts and set me straight.

"Down here, son, we have a saying. Horses sweat. Men perspire. Ladies glow."

Well, I had progressed from sweating to melting. Herb and Allan had briefly disappeared, but I saw the Dodge tow truck a few blocks down the street, outside the Florence Air and Missile Museum. I found them on the back verandah, sipping mint juleps and planning a manned mission to Mars with the head of the museum. Herb was wearing my Redskins cap and explaining exactly how to build the Martian Lander. I wondered if it would have a little flashing plastic rocket on the instrument panel.

I took advantage of the break to drain a tall iced tea, which delayed my meltdown. Then I bought a pair of black socks, which I hid under the truck seat for later use on the dashboard trophy.

We were back on the road in two hours, and as soon as Herb went back to sleep, I retrieved the socks and covered the blinking trophy, which I had quickly grown to despise—especially at night.

We crossed the border into Florida with me behind the wheel of the crew cab, Caroline attempting to read an enormous book of road maps beside me, and Herb snoring peacefully in the back seat.

"Why can't these map people draw?" she complained. "I mean, there must be 200 maps in this book, but do they ever stop to think that people might actually want to read these things? Eddie, which direction from this highway is Miami?"

"Thank you, Caroline."

She peeked over the top of the map at me.

"You're welcome. Now, do you know if we're heading anywhere near Miami, or is this a guy-thing about not needing directions?"

"I mean it. Thank you."

Caroline flattened the map onto her lap. She glanced over both shoulders and under her seat, searching for someone else in the truck before replying.

"Are we having the same conversation?"

"No, not yet," I replied.

"OK, let's start over. You go first," she offered.

"I was thinking about Toronto, about standing on top of that podium. That wouldn't have happened without you."

"You mean jumping over the fence back in California to rescue that driver?"

"That started it, but no, more than that. All those nights planning and organizing. And the race video, the artwork—"

"Don't forget the animal cookies," she reminded me.

"Right. Those too. You got me to stop and look around, to think about the team and not just myself. To see beyond the next green flag. Thanks for that. And thanks for being here now."

Caroline took all this in quietly. She stared out her window at the small farms and rolling countryside for a good minute before she turned back. I could feel those blue eyes studying me for several long moments.

"I made up my mind that you were worth it a long time ago, Eddie Stewart. You could be a goat herder, and I'd want to be around. This professional race-team thing is a bit more exciting than my art studio, and I know the guys believe that you can win more races. Maybe even have a shot at the championship. I think you can, too, and I'd like to be a part of it."

"I'd like that, too. I'd like that a lot," I said.

Chapter 20

Unfinished Business

The exquisite tenderness of this moment was shattered by a Star Wars blanket flying through the air from the back seat. Herb, who had exploded out of his semi-comatose state, was now sitting bolt upright behind me, with panic etched across his face. Caroline shrieked in surprise. I was stunned; this was a first. In all the years I'd known Herb, there was absolutely nothing that could awaken him when he was asleep. Until now. I wondered if he'd been attacked by a pack of rattlers in the back seat.

Or maybe he hadn't been asleep at all.

"Herb! What's going on?" I demanded.

The Man of Steel's breath came in short gasps and most of the color had drained from his face.

"Eddie…Caroline… Oh man…it was unbelievable! I…I just couldn't take any more!" he stammered.

Caroline retrieved Herb's blanket and put it around his shoulders.

"There's your blankie," she said. "Now, what's wrong? A nightmare?"

"No! It was worse… It was so real," Herb replied breathlessly. "I thought… I thought I was going to throw up."

I immediately slowed down and started to pull over to the shoulder of the highway.

"No, keep going, Eddie," Herb said. "I think I stopped it in time. It's over now."

"What's over?" I demanded.

Herb looked at the two of us, blinked innocently, and then grinned.

"Flaming romance! I just couldn't listen to you two up there cooing at each other like love birds anymore."

Caroline's attack was instant and furious as she pummeled Herb back into his seat with unrelenting blows from the map book. He roared with laughter as he deflected the assault, and Caroline and I eventually found ourselves joining in and laughing at our own expense as well.

Romance at short notice would have to wait. The final race in the Formula Atlantic series offered one last chance to go wheel-to-wheel with Raul DaSilva.

And maybe even to race for a championship. We had unfinished business waiting for us in Miami.

Caution period. A point when the race is slowed to allow the track to be cleared.

Champ Car. A formula race car competing in the Champ Car World Series.

Data acquisition. A computer system that collects information on race car performance.

Downforce. The load placed on a car by air flow over its front and rear WINGS.

Formula Atlantic. A single-seat, open-wheeled race car.

Gearbox. Contains gears that the driver shifts to transmit engine power to the wheels.

Grid. The starting lineup of cars, which is based upon qualifying times.

Marshals. Racetrack safety workers.

Oversteer. When the rear wheels lose their grip and a race car slides or spins.

Pace lap. A slow warm-up lap before starting the race.

Pace car. The official car that leads the race car field during the pace lap or caution period.

Paddock. The area where teams park transporters or set up garages.

Pit. The area where teams work on the race cars.

Pit Board. A sign that is held up by the pit crew to inform their driver of place, race position, and lap.

Push. Another term for UNDERSTEER.

Podium. A stage where the top three race finishers receive their awards.

Pole position. The first starting position, which is awarded to the fastest qualifier.

Qualifying. Timed laps that determine where each car will be positioned at the start of the race.

Rain tires. Deeply grooved, soft-compound tires that are designed for racing in the rain.

Setup. Adjustments that are made to the race car by crew members.

Slicks. Treadless racing tires.

Suspension. A system of springs, shocks, and levers that are attached to the wheels and support the race car.

Trans-Am. The Trans American Championship for modified sports cars.

Understeer. When the front wheels lose their grip and the race car continues straight rather than turning.

Wets. Another term for RAIN TIRES.

Wings. Direct airflow that passes over the race car, pushing it down onto the track.

ANTHONY HAMPSHIRE is as comfortable strapped into the seat of a race car as he is in front of a classroom. Raised in London, England, and Calgary, Alberta, Anthony has been a racing driver and team manager, a football coach, and a magazine columnist. He was also a classroom teacher and educational technology consultant and is now a school principal. Anthony has earned national and provincial awards for his work in school curriculum and media, authored educational software, and is a regular conference presenter and workshop leader. He makes his home at the foot of the Rocky Mountains in Alberta, where he lives with his wife, two daughters, and a bossy Welsh Corgi.

Crime
Cars